The Clearwater Union War

The Clearwater Union War

Ron Carter

Bookcraft
Salt Lake City, Utah

Library of Congress Catalog Card Number 99-72624
ISBN 1-57008-663-X

First Printing, 1999

Printed in the United States of America

CHAPTER 1

Big Ed scowled as he read the badly typed memo, then raised his head with lightning in his eyes.

"So them young punks think they're goin' to beat me in the next election, do they? Been to college and think they know everything. Think I'm a washed-up has-been. Well, ain't none of them knows gear-jammin' and eighteen-wheeler haulin' beef from New York to California without stoppin', and turnin' around the same day with a reefer loaded with lettuce headed back for New York. And they don't have no idee about how to talk to us who've done it, or how to persuade us good, experienced, professional, gentlemen truckers who to vote for in a union election. *Them's* the things you got to know to make this here union run, and they don't know nothin' about it, but *I do!*"

Big Ed rolled the ill-fated memo between his huge, thick palms into a tiny round ball and threw it disgustedly amongst the clutter on top of his heavy oak desk in his spacious, luxurious office at the top of the Tennison Building, the tallest on the Loop in downtown Chicago. From the south bank of windows one could see the sprawling city of Chicago spread for miles; from the north bank, the busy docks and the ships far below making white tracks on Lake Michigan. He slid his cold cigar from one corner of his mouth to the other and continued chewing one end to a pulp, massive jaw muscles flexing rhythmically while he glanced out the window at a beautiful, clear June morning.

Big Ed O'Rourke weighed 310. Thirty years ago, when he was the toughest truck driver in the AFL-CIO Union, he had stood six and a half feet tall and weighed 260. He missed a union meeting in the basement of Benny's Pool Hall on Chicago's south side one rainy Thursday night and, not being there to defend himself, was elected secretary of the local 422. Three months later the union treasurer for Cook County was found on the floor behind his office desk, deceased.

"Heart attack," ruled the Cook County coroner after looking at the dead treasurer's body on the office floor, "and he got those six big lumps on his head when he fell down after his heart stopped."

"He fell down six times after he was dead?" a skeptical homicide detective asked.

"Yeah," said the coroner. "Them truckers don't go down easy. It looks like that one was fallin' down and gettin' up for two, maybe three minutes after he died. Ain't no other way to explain it."

"How about someone whackin' him with that crowbar on the desk?"

The coroner stroked his jaw dubiously. "Naw, them truckers got heads like cannonballs. Wouldn't hardly notice gettin' whacked on the head by a crowbar."

This was Chicago, and the deceased was the treasurer of a union. That was enough to convince both the coroner and the detective of the deep wisdom in saying no more. By an unspoken agreement they closed their files, and the death was instantly forgotten.

Big Ed had nothing to do with the death, but he saw the possibilities offered by the fact that the position of union treasurer—the money man—was now open. For two weeks he had private talks with every union official in town, then finally got a letter in the mail: The union president had appointed him temporary treasurer until the next election.

They delivered the union account books to him. He threw four guys out of Benny's smoke-filled back room, where they played illegal card games, and for two days he laboriously added and subtracted the numbers in the right columns of the five pages while he chewed twenty-one cigars to death and drank three gallons of 7.6 percent dark Irish beer. When he had finished he carefully copied the final figure onto a piece of scrap paper and went down to the corner Greek deli and asked the Italian wife of Enrico to read it to him.

She counted the figures, closed her eyes and ticked it off on her fingers, then recited it to him. "Forty-one million three hundred twelve thousand dollars and seventy-seven cents." She cocked her head and narrowed her eyes. "Eduardo, for why do you want to know thees beeg number?"

She waited, but Big Ed did not speak or move; so she thrust her head forward and realized the pupils of his eyes were like pinpoints, and he was not breathing. She stepped to him, clapped her hands on his cheeks, and rubbed vigorously while she exclaimed, "Eduardo, Eduardo, speak, speak. If you are having the attack of the heart please to go outside to die so you do not scare off the customers."

Big Ed's eyes tried to focus. He swallowed, and his lips silently formed the words, "Forty-one muh-muh-muh-million?"

She clasped her hands together in relief. "You live! Si. Forty-one million. For why do you want to know . . ." Suddenly a thought struck her and she threw her hands in the air and exclaimed, "Mama mia! Eduardo, have you steal all the money from the government?"

Without a sound, Big Ed turned and walked out the door like a zombie. At noon the next day he was sitting locked in Benny's back room staring at the union books on the table before him when he again tried to make a sound. It came out in a low whisper that sounded much like a prayer. "Fuh-fuh-fuh-forty-one million dollars in the union trust account?" By four o'clock that afternoon he had dedicated the balance of his life to one single objective. He was going to be president of the union for the entire state of Illinois. By noon the next day he had filed his papers to run in the coming election, and by the next Monday he had his organization working like men possessed.

He won the election by a landslide when his opponent opted to withdraw from the race three days before the day of the voting. No one knew he had withdrawn; he simply failed to show up amid rumors that he had left suddenly to attend his father, who was dying in Sicily, Dublin, or Sydney, depending on who answered the telephone at his office. Within three days Big Ed moved the union headquarters from Benny's Pool Hall to its present location in the penthouse of the tallest, most luxurious building in Chicago. And he spent a million dollars of union money to redo and furnish it.

He had been reelected president at every election since then, mainly because he had shoulders like an ox, fists like hams, and Big Ed wasn't scared of nothing. Not the law, the United States Congress, nor the president of this fair land, who now happened to be Harry S. Truman. In at least four elections over the past three decades his opponents had quietly withdrawn from the race about a week before the day of the vote, when they found their automobiles smashed to smithereens and a big sign stuck on the gearshift that said VOTE FOR BIG ED.

One of his opponents, Roberto Carletti, who weighed only 225, swore he was going to beat Big Ed in the next election and clean up the union. Big Ed took indignant offense at that and visited Roberto's place around 2 A.M. When Roberto found his new Packard touring car ready for the junkyard the next morning he came looking for Big Ed, whom he found walking out of the union headquarters building onto the street. There was a brief but extremely intense discussion before Roberto lost his Italian temper and started to swing, but Big Ed got there first. There were just two hits: Big Ed hit Roberto, and Roberto hit the asphalt right there in the street, with two hundred wide-eyed people watching.

Self-defense, said Big Ed, and six white-faced Irish cops nodded vigorously. Yes, sir, Big Ed, there ain't no question about it. Self-defense.

Roberto didn't wake up for two days, and he spent the rest of the week trying to sort out who he was. He didn't mean to withdraw from the union election. He just couldn't remember that he belonged to the union, or that he was running for elective office.

But the years had taken their toll. Big Ed was slightly stooped; and his hair was nearly all gray, and it was thinning. His broad nose had been broken several times in hand-to-hand discussions, and now it permanently pointed slightly to his left. Whereas he used to be heavy in the neck and shoulders and arms, it all seemed to have settled to his middle. Lately he was having trouble finding his belt, which was tucked under his belly.

"Ferdie, get in here," he bellowed.

Ferdigo Alkanian came scooting from the outer office. "Yeah, Boss?"

Ferdie stood five feet six inches and, with a good breakfast, weighed about 120. His eyelids never raised over halfway, and his bushy eyebrows were always arched, which gave him the appearance of being extremely wise and judgmental. His face was thin, with a hawkish nose and a long upper lip, and his hair, once black and wavy, was now salt and pepper and wavy.

Ferdie had been with Big Ed since the first election, mainly because of his two great talents, most useful in running a union. There was no man in the entire organization who could sneak or eavesdrop like Ferdie, or who had so many shadowy connections into just about everything in Chicago. If Big Ed wanted to know what was in any document anywhere in Chicago, Ferdie would have a copy within twenty-four hours, no questions asked. If Big Ed wanted to know what anyone was saying to anyone, Ferdie would have the straight skinny on it by closing time the same day. If Big Ed needed a favor from anybody, from the mayor or the governor right down to the mobs who ran the numbers games and controlled the docks, he had only to mention it to Ferdie.

"Ferdie, I got a memo from the leaders of some of the locals. Heard about it?"

"Yeah, Boss."

Big Ed sobered and scrooched his big, round, heavy jowled face into a prune. "Any truth to it?"

"Dunno, Boss. Want I should find out?"

"Yeah. Find out. Meanwhile, I got some diggin' around to do."

Next morning Ferdie was waiting at 7:45 when Big Ed walked in.

"Yeah, Boss. There's truth to it." He pointed to a stack of photocopies on the desk. "Them is from the files of most of the locals, and they say the union's got to start lookin' legitimate, like a business, and to do that we got to elect a civic-minded president that ain't got no problems draggin' on him from the past. Clean, like one of them college kids. Rumors say most of the local chapters are thinkin' that way."

Big Ed's mouth narrowed and he settled silently into his big, overstuffed chair, which squeaked with his weight. Ferdie, knowing the look, walked out and closed the door, estimating he would hear from Big Ed in about an hour and a half. Meantime he sat down at his small desk in the corner of the anteroom to wait.

Irene, the receptionist, arrived at 8:30 and glanced at Ferdie. She quit chewing her gum long enough to ask, "So what's it with Big Ed today?" She drew a six-inch hat pin from the back of her twenty-inch, droopy-brim hat, hung the hat on a coat tree in one corner, and tugged at her girdle.

7

"A plan. He's workin' on a plan," Ferdie said.

She popped open her compact, dabbed powder on her nose, and jabbed at an errant strand of bleach-blond hair. "Good or bad?"

Ferdie shrugged.

Forty minutes later Big Ed opened his door, and Ferdie said to himself, "An hour and a half, right on the nose."

Big Ed stuck his head out. "Ferdie, come on in here."

Ferdie settled his sparse frame into a luxurious chair facing Big Ed's desk and waited. Big Ed's eyes were points of light, his face a blank. The cold cigar in one corner of his mouth had been chewed to a pulp.

"So that bunch of kids thinks Big Ed can't make it happen any more, huh? Well, what does Big Ed do when someone says that? Big Ed makes it happen some more. That's what he does." Big Ed looked bold.

Ferdie nodded. "Yeah, Boss."

"How does Big Ed do that?" Big Ed continued. "Easy. He organizes a few new chapters and adds them to the union. That's how he does it."

"Yeah, Boss."

"And this time, Big Ed does it so the whole union has to sit up and take notice. So how does he do that? He organizes a new chapter where there ain't never been no union before."

Ferdie's eyebrows raised a little higher. "Yeah, Boss. But where ain't there never been no union before?"

Big Ed looked superior. "I thought of that. I done some checkin' since yesterday." He opened one of the drawers of his big desk and withdrew a huge roll of paper. This he unrolled on his desk, anchoring the four corners with paperweights and an inkwell. Ferdie recognized it as a map of the Western Hemisphere. Big Ed thumped his finger down on Chicago and began sliding his finger west.

Ferdie peered intently at the upside-down map. The North Pole was nearest him, then the Dominion of Canada.

"Yer right, Boss. You organize Eskimos or Canadians, you'll sure get someone's attention."

"Come on, Ferdie," Big Ed growled. "We're going to organize a new chapter out in the West."

"Too late," Ferdie said. "Already got unions in Frisco and L.A."

"Not that far west," Big Ed said, showing pain. "Right here." He thumped his finger down.

Ferdie studied the map for a minute. "Idaho?"

"Yeah." Big Ed looked brilliant.

"Is that a state?"

"Yeah. Checked last night. Joined the U.S. back about 1890." Big Ed looked educated.

"They got electricity and phones and stuff out there?" Ferdie looked alarmed.

"A railroad and telegraph and electricity, the whole shebang."

"How many buffalo?"

Big Ed shrugged. "I don't know. But that's where we're sendin' Gino to organize a brand new chapter of the AFL-CIO."

"That looks like a big state. Which town?"

Big Ed nodded. "I gave that some thought, too." He looked crafty. "A little town named Hollis, right there, on that river. The Clearwater River. They got a meat-packing plant in that town, right on that river, run by a

9

local named Abe Jones. Calls it the Clearwater Meat Company. That meat plant is the central, main business in the whole area. So that's where we start. We get that meat plant organized, we got the whole central part of the state of Idaho. And within a month we'll spread out till we got the whole state."

Ferdie looked distressed. "Any Indian problem out there?"

Big Ed puckered his face. "Never thought of that." He scratched his jowl. "But I doubt it. They had soldiers in World War II, and the locals voted for Truman. Naw, they wouldn't have no Indian troubles."

"When do you figger to do all this?"

Big Ed looked efficient. "Two days. I got to send a letter to Jones first. Get Augie and Gino."

Ten minutes later Augie and Gino were standing in front of Big Ed's massive desk, beside Ferdie. Augie was five feet eight and weighed 260, wore a green pin-stripe, $29.98 suit, and parted his black hair down the middle. He had but one eyebrow, which ran from one side of his face to the other.

Gino was slightly shorter, swarthy, thin, hawk-faced, with a penciled mustache, wore a peach-colored pin-stripe suit, and had a constant twitch at the left corner of his mouth if he was required to stand still for over a minute or so.

"Yeah, Boss," Augie said through thick lips. His melon face was a blank.

Big Ed leaned back in his big, overstuffed chair. "Augie," he said, "you and Gino are going to organize a new chapter of the union for us. Gino does the negotiating and talking, and you do the persuading. Vinnie does all the book work and keeps minutes."

"Right, Boss," Augie answered.

Gino's face clouded. "Where?"

"In Idaho."

Gino's eyes bugged.

"Right, Boss," Augie said, and the expression of his face did not change.

Big Ed waited, and when Augie said nothing more Big Ed leaned forward and asked him, "You know where Idaho is?"

Augie brightened at being asked a question. "Down south, around Springfield somewhere?" he answered, hope springing in his eyes. "Springfield's the capital of Illinois," he added, smiling proudly.

"Criminy," Gino snorted, "he doesn't know nothin' from nothin'."

Big Ed sighed. "Idaho's out west." He unrolled the map and pointed. "Right there."

Augie studied the map for a minute and shook his head in deep thought. "They got any bars or restaurants out there?"

Gino threw both hands up. "Restaurants! Bars! All he ever thinks about!"

Big Ed ignored it. "You leave in two days."

"What kind of a union?" Gino exclaimed. "Hicks? Rednecks? We're goin' to be the laughin' stock. The first chapter of AFL-CIO Brothers of the Hick Rednecks in the U.S. of A." He shook his head.

"Watch your mouth," Big Ed warned. "I'll get to that."

"Do I drive the DeSoto?" Augie licked his lips in anticipation.

"No, you take the train."

"Just me and Gino alone?" Fear crept into his eyes.

"Naw, you'll need some extra persuaders. Take Dom and Tony and a couple more. Ferdie'll have your tickets. When you get there, rent a car. Ferdie'll give Gino written orders for the whole thing. Read 'em good."

Augie's eyes dropped and his face colored. "Boss, uh, you're forgetting something."

Big Ed rounded his lips and blew air, then said with resignation, "Yeah, right, okay. Gino, read the orders to him till he understands."

Gino grunted and looked disgusted.

Augie grinned. "Right, Boss."

Big Ed paused for emphasis, then turned directly to Gino. "You asked what kind of a union. You're going to organize a meat-cutters union at a meatpacking plant on the Clearwater River. It's owned and run by a local named Abe Jones."

Gino hunched his shoulders in surprise. "So what do we know about meat-cutters unions already? We don't know from nothin'!"

Big Ed frowned. "Then you start even with those pencil-necks out there, because they don't know from nothin' about unions neither."

Gino sadly shook his head.

"So Augie," Big Ed continued, "who do you want to take, besides Dom and Tony?"

Augie thought for a moment. "Franco and Guiseppe. Do we get to take our hardware? Maybe even a tommy gun or two?" He looked hopeful.

12

Big Ed puckered while he thought. "Yeah, take 'em but don't shoot nobody. Just let people see 'em enough to get the idea it'd be smart to join." He turned to Ferdie. "Write out the orders and get the train tickets ready for these guys."

"Yeah, Boss."

"Okay. You three get outta here and get busy." He raised his head and shouted, "Irene, you out there?"

"Whaddaya think already? Like I'm on the subway maybe!" came her high, piercing answer.

"Get a pencil and pad for a letter."

"In a minit," came the answer.

"What's the holdup?"

"Workin' on my stockings. They're crooked. You want I should look like somethin' cheap, off the streets maybe?"

Big Ed closed his eyes and shook his head as Ferdie, Augie, and Gino walked out.

Five minutes later Irene swivelled through the door, sat down in a chair at the corner of the desk nearest Big Ed, and flashed her biggest smile.

"Okay, Eddie Baby," she said, "what do you want I should write?"

"Take a letter. To Abe Jones, Clearwater Meat Company, Hollis, Idaho."

Irene fluttered her false black eyelashes. "Now, slow down, Eddie Baby," she said. "How do you spell Abe?"

"A B E."

She worked for several seconds, erased twice, added something, then smiled sweetly. "How do you spell Jones?"

CHAPTER 2

Abe Jones paused at the front door of the tired old slab-sided, unpainted building for just a moment, and glanced eastward at the sky above the jagged peaks of the great Rocky Mountains. A sun not yet risen had magically transformed the light clouds to a glorious symphony of reds and yellows and pinks, and while Abe watched, the first tiny, hesitant arc of sun crested the peaks. Light flooded down the valley and turned the emerald green pines to gold, and the Clearwater River to a twisting ribbon on the valley floor.

He hitched at the shoulder straps on his overalls, filled his lungs with clean, crisp June morning air, and listened to the jays and meadowlarks welcoming the new, beautiful, rare day. He smiled and looked at the cracked, faded, homemade sign nailed on the wall beside the door:

CLEARWATER MEAT COMPANY
Abe & Beth Jones, Props.

Abe stood an even six feet and weighed about 150. His thick, wavy hair was snowy white, and the seams and ridges and hollows of his craggy, weather-tanned face were a road map of life's battles. The light and fight still shined in his sharp, clear, blue eyes, and the smile wrinkles far outnumbered the frowners. His arms were a little too long, and hung loose, and gave him a slight "Ichabod" feel. His strong hands were huge and the knuckles too large, and they showed a life of hard work with the meat business, fishnets, and the good earth. A large Roman nose dominated his face, and his square jaw and chin lent a stubborn aura.

"Got to repaint that sign," he mumbled to himself, as he had done nearly every morning for the past ten years.

The weathered old building had survived hot summers and the deep snows of the Rocky Mountain winters for forty years. Tumbledown log corrals and pens joined it on the north and west sides, for holding stock brought to be processed. An oversized smokehouse stood on the east side, for smoking anything brought in by neighbors and customers for eighty miles in every direction. That included fish, beef, pork, venison, elk, moose, bear, ducks, geese, pheasant, quail, and about a ton of German sausages brought in every fall by the Hutterites, who had their little community twelve miles north. Forty tons of dried applewood was stacked twenty feet east of the smokehouse, the last remains of Zumwald's old orchard that went to ruin after Herman Zumwald died. Applewood smoked sweet, and Abe's smokehouse was famous all up and down the river.

Abe had a small, regular route of meat customers thirty miles in both directions, and he processed enough of his own meat to make a delivery once a week in each direction in his pickup truck. His main business was custom processing animals for just about everybody on the river. They brought in their own livestock, he

15

processed it in any way they said, and they picked it up later, or he delivered for an extra dollar. He charged money for his services when he could, bartered when he couldn't, traded meat for work with half a dozen men up and down the river, and swapped one kind of meat for another when there was need. If anybody needed cash money for a good reason, Abe could usually scare up a few dollars for them, and swap a pig or a day's work for it.

Eighty feet to the south, the Clearwater River ran its eternal course to the Snake, and on to the Pacific Ocean. It was clear and sweet and seasonally filled with salmon and trout that Abe, and everyone else on the river, took with nets or lines and smoked for winter.

For a moment Abe listened to the steady hum of the big, fifty-horsepower electric motor that lifted river water up to the five-thousand-gallon holding tank on top of the old building. Without an abundance of good water there would be no Clearwater Meat Company.

Abe's hand-built log home stood in pine trees two hundred feet further north, just beyond the county road that followed the river. The road was rutted dirt, dusty in the summer, muddy in the spring and fall, and frozen in the winter.

Beth, his wife of forty years, kept the home neat as a pin and also managed the books for the meat company. The books consisted of her carefully written notes in a single cloth-bound ledger. She kept a running account of what they sold to their own few customers, which neighbor brought in what livestock to be processed, and the deal she or Abe made to do it. There wasn't a debit or credit column in the entire ledger.

Beth was as round and plump as Abe was tall and gangly. No one could ever remember her not smiling. And no one within fifty miles could remember ever having sickness or calamity that Beth heard about without her showing up with supper from her oven. When she smiled at Abe he still blushed and stammered, notwithstanding their forty years of marriage and four good children raised, married, and gone. Three still lived on the river. Elvie, the youngest daughter, had moved to Boise with her husband, who worked as an engineer for the state.

The battered old office door creaked when Abe opened it, and he walked through the office, on through the meat-cutting room, past the cooler and drip room to the boiler room and fired the boiler. Mattie Linderman had brought in six large gilts yesterday, to be made into ham, bacon, lard, and sausage, so they had to be done today. Processing pigs took a lot of hot water, and Abe would have it ready by seven o'clock, when Elbert and Charlie and Al were supposed to show up to help.

Today it was Elbert and Charlie and Al, but tomorrow it would be Gene and Jack. Next week it would be Jim and Bill. He rotated according to availability and the job to be done. When the crew weren't working at the plant, they were busy putting in or weeding or harvesting a vegetable garden, getting game, pulling fish out of the river, fixing up their places or their pickup trucks.

He watched the needle on the steam gauge jiggle and then start its slow, steady climb before he walked back to the office. He stopped long enough to look at the ledger, to see when Mattie wanted to pick up the fresh sausage. Then he walked on out into the morning air and started towards home, where Beth would have steaming pancakes and hot sausages waiting.

He heard the sound of the old Chevy pickup engine before it drove into view, and he slowed at the road to watch it rattle to a stop in front of him. U.S. MAIL had been painted on the passenger door with a stick and white paint. The glass had been smashed out of the window seven years earlier when Buster Fieldman, the mail deliveryman for the River Route, ran off the road in a bad rainstorm and rolled the truck over twice in the barrow pit. Abe and Buster and a few others tipped it back onto its wheels, and Buster cranked it up. It clattered a lot, but it still ran, and nobody paid much attention to the missing window or the cracks in the windshield, or the dents on both sides and the top. Buster never did take it in for repairs. He stuck a sheet of plywood in the window hole during bad weather and kept right on driving.

Buster was just past thirty, intense, corpulent, thinning hair, and a bachelor. He had faithfully courted Betty Bottoms for four years after high school before she ran off with a seed salesman, and Buster had never again sought the affections of another woman. No, sir, Betty was his one and only true love, and someday she would see her mistake and return to him. In the meantime he would sacrifice the best years of his life while he remained forever true and faithful to his Betty. Two years earlier a travelling preacher said he'd seen Betty down south of the Snake River, with seven kids, another one coming, and the seed salesman somewhere else selling seeds.

Buster shook his head. No, sir, that ain't my Betty, because she's coming back pretty soon, and I'm going to wait. And so far, he had waited.

Abe grasped the windowsill on the passenger side. "Howdy, Buster," he said. "Up early. Better pull in over there and come on in for some pancakes and sausage."

"That'll have to wait. I got important mail."

"Yeah? For who?"

"You."

Abe's eyes widened. "What is it?"

Buster's forehead wrinkled. "Don't rightly know. Got this funny circle sort of thing in one corner, looks sort of like Nazis." He handed the envelope to Abe.

Abe glanced at both sides, then slowly read his name and address, and then the return address in the upper left corner, and examined the circled symbol of the union.

"AFL-CIO AMALGAMATED UNION," he read. "Penthouse, Tennison Building, Chicago, Illinois."

He cocked one eyebrow at Buster. "Ever heard of an AFL-CIO Amalgamated Union?"

Buster raised his ample chin and scratched underneath. "Nope. I heard of the FBI and I heard of FDR and RIP, but I don't know nothin' about no AFL or CIO."

Abe shook his head. "It's from Chicago, so I doubt it's from the Nazis. Naw, it couldn't be the Nazis, because we whupped them four years ago in Europe."

Suddenly Buster froze and his face went white. "It's communists! That's what that is. Harry S. Truman's been on the radio tellin' us to watch for them communists because they're fixin' to take over America. And here we got 'em comin' right out to get us! I better report this to Alice."

Alice was the telephone operator in Lewiston, twenty-eight miles southwest. If anything happened on the River Route that looked wrong, or bad, Buster reported it to Alice. She had an organization of women that had telephones, including the sheriff's office and the newspaper, and what those women couldn't fix in about twenty minutes just didn't need fixing. The men thought they were running the county; Alice's underground network never did tell them otherwise, but let them live on in their bliss and ignorance. The local radio station owner, Lou Gibney, had long since learned that Alice's switchboard was the crossroads of everything about everybody, and he called her a time or two each day to get the latest on whose kids had the chicken pox, and whose cow had birthed a calf, and who had run off with whose wife.

Buster figured having Nazis or communists sending mail right down there on the river was the worst thing since Pearl Harbor, and Alice had to know. What Buster didn't know was that twenty years ago when he and Alice were in the fourth grade together, he had changed her life forever. She challenged him to a marble game during recess and she beat him, so he whopped her in the stomach and knocked the wind out of her and she fainted. When she woke up, she was in love with him forever. Being naturally ladylike, she never told anyone; but in all those years when Buster had been waiting for Betty, Alice had secretly been waiting for Buster.

Buster had always thought it real neighborly of Alice to show up at his house with homemade berry pies twice a month, and he never did figure out who left home-knitted socks and sweaters and mittens on his doorstep every Christmas. And he was too moonstruck over Betty to detect the quaver in Alice's voice every time he talked to her. But most of all, Buster had never looked inside himself to question why he always, without fail, thought of calling Alice first when things, good or bad, big or little, suddenly came up. He had always told himself it was because her telephone switchboard was the crossroads of the world and she'd know who to call.

"Maybe we ought to read the letter inside first," Abe said.

Buster puckered his face for a minute. "Well, okay, but we can't take much time because it'll take an hour to get back to Alice." Buster parked the old, faded-blue pickup in front of the house and followed Abe inside. Abe gestured to the breakfast table and they both sat down. Abe slit open the envelope with a knife and began to read.

"That you?" Beth called from the kitchen.

"Yep, and Buster's here. Put on some more pancakes and sausages."

"Howdy, Buster," came the cheerful voice. "Right nice to have you stop. Say, you're pretty early. Everything okay?"

"No ma'am, we got a national emergency goin' here."

Beth appeared in the doorway, silently waiting for his explanation.

"Genuine Chicago Nazis or communists!"

Beth gasped, clapped her hand over her mouth, and her eyes popped. "Oh mercy me!" she exclaimed. Then she sniffed the air, quickly turned back into the kitchen, and rapidly cleared ten plate-sized pancakes from the griddle onto a platter. She walked back to the breakfast table and set them down, with a large pitcher of hot syrup, and Buster speared five pancakes onto his plate with one jab of his fork.

"How do you know?" she asked Buster.

He carved large hunks of butter off the big ball Beth had churned and set in a bowl, and expertly shoved the chunks between the pancakes.

"Why," he said, "it's all right there in that letter I just gave to Abe. Drove out special when I seen who it was from."

Beth walked back into the kitchen and reappeared with a heaping plate of smoking sausages and a steaming pot of coffee. She looked at Abe. "What does it say?"

Buster grasped the big pitcher and lifted each pancake long enough to drown the stack in homemade maple syrup.

Abe looked thoughtful. "Don't know yet. I'm just reading it now."

Buster palmed four six-inch sausage patties onto his plate. "I seen that symbol up there in the corner of that envelope," he said as he made his first cut into the tender, smoking pancakes, "and I knowed right off it was either Nazis or communists." He stuffed the first forkload into his mouth and commenced chewing.

Beth waited.

Abe finished reading.

"Well," Beth said quietly, "what does it say?"

Abe leaned back, puzzled. "I ain't rightly sure. It sounds like they want us to join the union."

Buster choked and swallowed hard, then quickly drank from his coffee cup. "President Lincoln already done that, in the Civil War."

Beth smiled. "No, he *saved* the union in the Civil War. Idaho joined the union in 1890."

Buster's nose wrinkled. "All the same, we already belong to the union and we can't join it twice. What the communists wants is for us to join *their* union." Half a sausage patty disappeared into his mouth.

"Better eat your breakfast, Abe," Beth said. "You got a crew comin' pretty soon."

Abe nodded and reached for the pancakes. "Take a look at it, Beth, and see what you think."

Beth read while the men ate.

"Some union men are already on their way," she said.

"Why?" Abe asked.

Beth shrugged. "It doesn't say."

"What's that AFL-CIO stuff all about?"

Beth shook her head. "I don't know. The government's getting like alphabet soup. FBI, G-men, soldiers are GIs, Roosevelt is now FDR—land-a-livin' they're usin' up all the letters."

Buster's eyes narrowed in suspense. "They're sendin' communists *here?*"

Beth thought for a moment. "It doesn't say communists. Just men to talk about the union."

Buster bolted down the last of the pancakes and stood. "We ain't got no time to waste. I got to get back and tell Alice. Much obliged for the breakfast, Beth." He jammed the last two sausages into his jacket pocket and marched out the door.

Abe thoughtfully finished his breakfast. "When does that letter say those men are going to get here?"

Beth glanced at it. "Tomorrow or the next day."

Abe nodded and headed for the door. "I better get on over to the plant. Elbert'll be coming soon."

He walked back down to the plant and checked the boiler. The steam pressure was up, and the water was hot. He changed from his high-topped shoes to his black, knee-high rubber boots, slipped into his stiff, yellow rubber apron, and buckled on his belt with the knife scabbard on his right side. He was rolling up the sleeves of his old, red-checked, faded shirt when he heard the rattle and clatter of Elbert's pickup truck coming in to park near the smokehouse.

Everybody on the river drove a pickup. They were mostly old, dented, weather-faded red or blue, and there was a never-ending argument whether Fords beat Chevys in the Clearwater mountains. The Chevy people argued that Fords always had some little thing going wrong and they'd nickel-and-dime you to death, while the Ford people argued Chevys were too cold-blooded in the winter and hard to start. A couple of times the arguments got hot, and once Sarah Mullens had whacked Abby Buxton over the head with a piece of quilting frame at a church social when Abby looked at Sarah's quilt and stuck her nose in the air and grunted, "Humphh, what else can you expect from someone who drives a Ford."

Nobody could ever remember a pickup on the Clearwater, Ford or Chevy, that didn't have a gunrack mounted in the back window, loaded with weapons. Usually a .22 for plugging gophers and rabbits, and a heavier rifle for deer and elk, or an occasional bear. There was almost always a shotgun for pheasants or quail, and ducks and geese, and a gunbelt and holster with a pistol. There were laws regulating hunting seasons, but folk on the river depended on game for their tables and took it when they could.

Hooter Yount, the game warden, had long since found out there was no way to stop it, and he gave up, except that he kept his eyes peeled for people from California. They all seemed rich and didn't mind paying the $300 fee for nonresident permits, and besides they were all crazy and dangerous, so far as he could tell. Two California hunters had shot Bert Wooley's Holstein cow once during deer season, and Hooter got so mad he locked both hunters in the basement of the Moose Lodge in Lewiston for two nights because the jail was under repairs, and he made them pay Bert $100 for the cow. Killing the cow wasn't what made Hooter mad. It was the fact that six-year-old Bobby was milking it in a pen beside the barn when they shot it.

Anybody, boy or girl, old enough to scramble into a pickup knew how to shoot all kinds of guns, and anybody above twelve years old could hit a running deer with a Winchester at 100 yards, a running rabbit with a .22 at 30 yards, and a flying anything at 50 yards with a shotgun. Anyone over fifteen could stand flat-footed for an hour and never take a deep breath while they spun wonderful shooting stories, and they all ended by swearing they were the honest, gospel truth.

Old Zeb Hawkins was recognized as having the best gun story of all, and he'd told it every chance he got for thirty years, before he died. He swore he'd killed a grizzly with his trusty old .22, with a 4,000-yard shot. Yessir, right smack between the eyes, which was the onliest place he could shoot the bear with that little bitty gun, and kill it. Amos Bailey scoffed and shook his head, but Zeb swore to it.

So Amos looked it up and found out there were only 1,760 yards in a mile, and then he spent a day writing a letter to the Remington Arms Company and asked them what was the longest distance a .22 bullet would go. The answer was, not much over 2,000 yards, maximum, shooting downwind. Amos waited until Zeb was telling the story again at a horseshoe contest, and announced real loud: "Them bullets won't go half that far. I got the proof right here in a letter from the Remington company that makes 'em."

Zeb choked on that for about half an hour and then suddenly recollected that it was a downhill shot, yessir, down a steep mountainside, and shootin' down like that the bullet would go 4,000 yards easy.

Amos blinked and thought for ten minutes, and then asked Zeb, Which mountain? Ain't no mountain in these parts that's 4,000 yards up.

Zeb scratched his head and screwed his face up like a prune, as though he was reaching a long way back into his memory, and said, tarnation, that shot mighta been in Alaska when I was up there pannin' for gold. They got plenty of 4,000-yard mountains up there. But he couldn't rightly remember because it was so long ago.

Then Zeb died, and a year later Amos died, and the preacher at Amos's funeral opined those two old liars were probably together again, still arguing over that

4,000-yard shot, without mentioning exactly *where* they were now continuing to argue.

Any man over sixteen could fix any part of a Ford or Chevy pickup, and every truck had a few wrenches and screwdrivers and pliers under the seat for emergencies. Nearly anyone of age could pull out a transmission and fix it in one day, or the entire engine, and fix any crankshaft, valve, con rod, piston, or cylinder in two. Every dooryard on the river had an old wreck sitting not too far from the house that was used for spare parts, because ten bucks for an old wreck that was a treasure of spare parts was a lot cheaper than a twenty-eight-mile drive to Lewiston every time something went wrong, and besides, you had to pay cash for each part in Lewiston.

"Abe, you in there?" Elbert Pike's lusty shout rang down across the river. He strode from his pickup towards the meat plant, and he broke out in a raucous chorus of "Jack of Diamonds" when he was halfway there.

"Rye whiskey, rye whiskey, rye whiskey I cry,

"If I don't get rye whiskey I surely will die."

He threw the front door open and walked through the office into the meat-cutting room. "Abe," he bellowed, "you got the water hot?"

"Yeah. Back here. Seen Charlie or Al?"

"Nope." Elbert walked back to the boiler room where they all hung their work gear on pegs, and pulled off his shoes while Abe stood nearby, sharpening the round-domed scrapers used to remove the hair from hogs. Elbert resumed his song in his loud, abandoned, twangy, nasal baritone while he put on his rubber boots.

"If the ocean was whiskey and I was duck,

"I'd dive to the bottom and never come up."

"Jack of Diamonds, Jack of Diamonds, Jack of Diamonds, I cry,

"If I don't get rye whiskey I surely will die."

He grinned at Abe while he tied on his yellow rubber apron. "You're lookin' awful sober this mornin'. Beth finally come to her senses and run you off?"

Elbert was the most complicated man on the river. He stood five feet ten inches in his stockinged feet and weighed 187 pounds stripped to the waist. He was heavy and muscled and strong as a bull in the shoulders and arms, and narrow in the hips. His nose was prominent, he had a jaw like stone, and he was considered handsome in a rugged way. He could do almost anything he set his mind to, and some things he did better than anyone else. He was generally genial and open and loud, showed respect for women and loved kids, but could be quiet and thoughtful and humble when the occasion required. He drank occasionally, caroused occasionally, went to church and repented occasionally, and nearly always took the part of the underdog in a showdown.

Three years earlier, when the summer league softball tournament got rowdy in Lewiston, they sent for Elbert to umpire. Elbert didn't know much about umpiring softball, but when the troublemakers started throwing empty beer cans in the third inning he pulled off his umpire's mask and walked around the wire backstop where about fifteen of the rowdies stood ready and waiting. When he finished, six of them were on the ground, and the other nine were in the bleachers, where they silently watched the last six innings before they gathered up their fallen comrades and left.

He was his own man. When things were wrong according to his notions, he was fearless in setting them right, and that included the law. If a law was dumb, he ignored it. No one ever had a more loyal friend or worse enemy.

It was pretty much agreed that Elbert could hit harder and quicker with his fists than anyone else within five hundred miles. He was no bully, but when he decided to set things right, or someone started something, he had thunder and lightning in both hands, and no one could remember him ever losing a fight.

Four years ago, Caleb Bender had hired Elbert to dig his potato crop, but the pickers refused to come pick them after Elbert got the first twenty acres dug. "They want four cents a sack," Caleb explained, "even though the contract says three. I can't pay the extra. They got me over a barrel."

Elbert walked into the first bunkhouse, where twelve pickers were waiting, and told them they better honor their contract. They all shook their heads no, and Elbert hit the first one. Three minutes later the bunkhouse was a wreck, seven of them were on the floor, four of them were outside setting a world speed record in picking potatoes, and the last one—the one that pulled the knife and opened a four-inch cut on Elbert's right cheek and another cut six inches long on his right forearm—was lying outside in the wreckage of the window through which Elbert had thrown him when he found out which man had pulled the knife. The window had been closed at the time.

When they heard the crash and saw a man come sailing through the closed window, and saw the still bodies strewn all over the bunkhouse, all twelve potato-pickers in the next bunkhouse ran to the field and joined the four already working. Elbert had Caleb stitch up his arm with a sacking needle and some fish line, and that afternoon when he finished digging for the day, Elbert drove to Lewiston, where a veterinarian put eighteen stitches in the deep cut on his face. The potato-pickers didn't stop picking until midnight, and they finished the whole job two days ahead of schedule.

Abe finished sharpening the hog scraper and grinned at Elbert. "Naw, nothing like that. I got a letter this morning from Chicago. Seems like they want to talk to me about joining a union."

Elbert grinned his infectious grin. "Join the union? Save your confederate money; the South will rise again. Someone's trying to start the Civil War all over."

They walked out the door, to the pen holding the pigs. "I don't think so," Abe mused. They both looked up at the sound of Charlie's old pickup approaching.

Charlie Hallenberger was old and dried up; his eyes always looked tired, and his smile nearly sad. He had seen action in the Argonne in World War I, survived mustard gas, spent two years in a hospital getting well, come home, married Evelyn, raised a son and a daughter, and now worked off and on at the plant. He brought back a German Lugar pistol as a war souvenir, was spinning it on his finger one night when it accidentally went off. The bullet caught him at the point of his jaw, travelling upward, and came out of his scalp just above his ear. The wound wasn't serious but it took something out of old Charlie, and he never moved fast after that, and he never wanted much more than to be left alone. He drank when he could get it, which irked Evelyn awful, and when he came home drunk, she'd smack him a good one and put him to bed.

New Year's Eve three years ago, someone dropped off a quart of Jack Daniels as a gift to the crew at the meat plant, and after they finished work at noon Charlie started nipping and didn't quit until he was drunk. Al and Elbert took him home to his shack on the old dump ground road. Evelyn met them at the door and helped Charlie inside, while Elbert and Al stood quietly on the dirt outside and listened. Sure enough, they heard the whop, and then old Charlie hit the wall, and then everything was peaceful.

Evelyn was a pretty good sort of woman, with one or two minor flaws. She was four inches taller than Charlie, eighty pounds heavier, hated it when Charlie drank, wished he had more ambition, and hated taking baths. She forced herself to take one the first day of every month, usually in cold water, but by around the twenty-second of the month no one needed to be told when Evelyn was within four hundred yards. Sitting in church with her after the tenth of the month became a study in bench selection. Even outdoors, anybody that had to stand and talk to her developed great skill in getting upwind without making it too obvious. And she never seemed to change her shapeless, faded blue dress. Rumor was that she wore it even when she took her monthly bath.

"Howdy," Charlie said. He went to put on his apron and boots. Al came right behind, and in five minutes the four of them were silently settled into the job.

Shackle 'em, hoist 'em, stick 'em, scald 'em, scrape 'em, shave 'em, hang 'em, eviscerate 'em, split 'em, wash the carcass clean with cold water, into the drip cooler while it cooled, then into the big cooler, where it chilled overnight to thirty-four degrees.

They hit their rhythm and moved steadily and silently through the six pigs. Charlie was the one that operated the two-wheeled metal wagon into which all the entrails were dumped. He saved the kidneys and the liver and the connecting tissue for rendering, and dumped the rest into a tank to be cooked for fertilizer and animal feed. The saying was, they used everything but the squeal.

Tomorrow they would cut the carcass into hams, bacon, loins, shoulders, jowls, trim the fat for the rendering, brine-pump and salt it all down in pickling vats except four of the loins, grind the sausage trimming, render the lard, and wrap the head separate because Mattie made good head cheese. Mattie would come in the next day for the fresh-packaged sausage, the four loins that were cut into pork chops and packaged, and the wrapped head. Four weeks from now she would pick up all the smoked meat and buckets of lard, which would last until midwinter.

They were finished by twelve-thirty, and by one o'clock had washed the place down with steam hoses.

They went to the boiler room to change out of their work clothes.

"I passed Buster comin' in this morning," Al said to Abe as he pulled on his lace-up shoes. "What's this about a communist invasion?"

"Naw, Buster just gets excited. Some men are supposed to come in the next couple days to talk about a union. I don't have any idea why."

Al worked on his shoelaces. Al Pardo was short, wiry, wise to the ways of life on the Clearwater, and a strong worker. Despite his diminutive size, Al used a seven-inch skinning knife for skinning beef instead of the standard six-inch blade, because he was strong in his wrists. No one could take off a beef hide like Al, and no one could remember the last time he scored a hide. When Al dropped a hide, it was near perfect.

He loved raising hunting dogs. He kept dog kennels and had won two blue ribbons and one red ribbon at local gundog trials over the years, with his prize short-haired German pointer, Bismarck. He always had two or three good hunters around that he would rent out if he knew the people, or go with the people and work the dogs if he didn't know them. For that he charged double, and people were usually glad to pay it. He also had a yard dog named Turk that was about seventeen years old, blind in one eye, had at least twelve different bloodlines, the rattiest coat in the state, and the sourest temper. Turk was too old and short of fang to do much damage, and moved much too slow, but could still set up a racket that would stop strangers at fifty yards.

They all hung their gear on the wall pegs by the boiler, and Abe led them out to the office, where Beth had slabs of roast beef between slices of homemade bread and butter, with a little watercress added, homemade dill pickles, a two-quart Kerr jar full of fresh milk, and a fresh blueberry pie waiting. While they ate, Beth made her entries in the ledger.

33

Al finished and wiped his mouth. "Good vittles, Beth. Thanks." He looked at Abe. "I can't hardly imagine what this union thing's all about. Let me know, will you?"

CHAPTER 3

Gino hunched forward in the front seat of the faded black 1938 Packard hearse, intently watching the rutted gravelled road ahead. The nervous tick jerked at the left corner of his mouth.

"Criminy," he lamented. "An hour on this crummy road and whadda we got? Nothin'. Beatin' this junk heap to pieces, and—nothin'!" He threw both hands in the air and flopped back against the seat in resignation.

"Maybe there ain't no such town as Hollis," Augie said quietly as he tried to maneuver the hearse around the potholes. "Maybe Big Ed read the map wrong."

"Yeah, right already," Gino snapped. "So *you* call Chicago and tell him. Big Ed, you stupid or somethin'? We hit every pothole in every lousy road in the state of Idaho huntin' for the town of Hollis, and there ain't no such town. Yeah, *you* call him."

Vinnie, seated between Augie and Gino, hunched forward and examined the map spread on his briefcase. He pushed his thick glasses back up his nose and squinted out the windshield. "Isn't that a town?" He pointed through the cracked windshield.

Gino lunged forward, hope springing, then flopped back again. "You should be a Boy Scout already," he exclaimed. "That's two cows in some trees."

35

Vinnie squinted harder and shrugged. "I was just asking."

Franco, Dom, and Guiseppe, jammed in the backseat, sat silently in a sort of contained rage. Behind them, in the space reserved for the casket, Tony lay out full length among all the suitcases, trying to see past the six heads in front of him, all wearing wide-brimmed, black felt hats with wide hatbands.

Ferdie had arranged train tickets to Boise, Greyhound bus tickets north to Lewiston, and enough money to rent a car in Lewiston for a week for the twenty-eight-mile ride to Hollis, where they were to rent motel rooms. But the Greyhound office in Boise had bad news: The route north to Lewiston had been temporarily closed because of heavy road repairs on White Bird grade, where a cloudburst had wiped out two hairpin turns. They could wait one day and take a bus through Oregon, up to Spokane, and come back down to Lewiston. That would take three more days.

"Fergit it," Gino said, and went to the Chrysler dealer in Boise.

"We want to rent a DeSoto limo."

"Fine," the salesman said, and took them to the owner.

"Uh, that's fine," the balding fat man said, "but we don't rent cars. We sell them. We don't handle limousines. A new DeSoto costs $5400. For you, I got a deal. Forty-nine hundred cash, no questions asked."

Gino's head thrust forward. "Don't rent cars? So what are you guys, pilgrims?"

The man looked over his glasses. "You need a car for just a short time?"

"Yeah. Like a week only."

"Hummm," the man said, looking at their pin-stripe suits and colored shirts and ties. "Tell you what. What you want to do is buy a reliable used car, use it for a week, and return it here. I'll buy it back from you at the price you paid, less a fair charge for the week's use. How's that?"

Gino considered. "In writin'? Guaranteed in writin'?"

"Of course."

"No limos?"

"No. But I have just the vehicle for you. Big enough to carry all of you and your baggage."

"Yeah, like what?" Gino snorted. "A truck already?"

"No. Step right this way."

They all followed the man, who led them to the used car lot and pointed.

Gino exploded. "A used 1938 Packard *hearse?* So whadda we look like, dead?"

Half an hour later he had stopped fuming long enough to lay $300 in cash on the man's desk, and to take the written guarantee of a buyback within eight days and jam it into his wallet.

With Vinnie tracing backroads on a map with his finger, and giving orders to Augie at the wheel, they had worked their way north, and got to Lewiston a day and a half late. They had stopped for gas and to get a flat tire patched, and asked the service station attendant for directions. He looked at the hearse, with its bronze letters "Peabody Mortuary" still in the side windows and seven men in pin-stripe suits and felt hats, swallowed hard, shoved his oil-stained baseball cap back and pointed with a grease blackened finger.

37

"Hollis? Oh yeah, sure, right, sure thing. Take the first gravel road right down yonderway, and keep goin' till you hit it. Just follow the river. Can't miss."

That had been an hour ago. They had stopped to stretch their legs, and now, ten minutes after getting back in the car, they rounded a curve and Gino's head dropped forward. Ahead, just off the road, was a building with a sign above the door.

"Pull over there," he ordered Augie, "and ask directions."

Augie obediently pulled off the gravelled road and stopped in front of the square frame building. Flakes of thirty-year-old white paint still clung here and there, and none of the four walls were in plumb. The front window had unreadable remains of red lettering on the inside and a crooked strip of black tape holding a crack together. The faded, cracked sign above the door said "Feeney's Groc."

Inside, Guy Feeney heard the hearse slow and the brakes whine as it stopped. He peered out through the grimy window and narrowed his eyes in disbelief. "Emma, better come see this," he called over his shoulder. As he spoke his Adam's apple bobbed and moved his four-day growth of white whiskers.

Emma waddled through the curtain that divided the store from their living quarters at the rear and made her way through the clutter and jumble of dry goods, canned food, farm tools, guns, ammunition, and the stand-up beer cooler. She stopped at the front window.

"Well I swan!" she murmured under her breath. "Who died?"

"Dunno," Guy answered. "But that's a genuine hearse. Ever hear of an undertaker named Peabody?"

"Not nowhere on the river."

They watched the door open and Augie climb out, followed by the others.

Guy's eyes bugged. "What in this green world is *that?*"

Emma clapped her hand over her mouth. "I seen that awful picture of that Valentine's Day killing in Detroit or Chicago or somewhere, and the dead men looked just like that, with them pin-striped suits and them hats and all." She went white as a sheet. "Are those men Detroit gangsters come here with dead bodies in a hearse, or maybe to kill a whole slew of us and put *in* the hearse? Oh heavens, Guy, what'll we do?" She started to tremble.

Guy rounded his lips and blew air for a second, then hastened to the gunrack and deftly loaded a double-barreled shotgun and handed it to Emma, along with six extra shells. "We'll go down fightin', that's what we'll do." He jammed shells into the magazine of a Remington shotgun, pumped one into the chamber, shoved a handful of shells into his sweater pocket, thrust out his chin, and walked to the front door.

"Emma," he said valiantly, "you go on in the back room and hide under the bed. If they get past me, you hold out as long as you can, and then—save the last shot for yourself. Gangsters lust after women and do bad things. Don't let 'em git you."

Emma turned and quickly waddled back into their living quarters. At 280 pounds there was no chance of her hiding under the bed without raising one side about a foot off the floor, so she hid behind the dresser and hoped Guy wouldn't think badly of her if he ever found out she didn't do what he said.

When nobody came out of the store, Augie walked to the door and was reaching for the bent knob when Guy jerked it open from the inside; and the next thing Augie knew, he was looking down the bore of a twelve-gauge Remington semiautomatic shotgun. Augie stood stone still, eyes popping out of his head, and stared into the two steely gray eyes at the other end of the shotgun barrel. Vinnie ducked back behind the hearse. All the others shoved their right hands inside their double-breasted coats and waited for Gino's signal.

"All right," Guy exclaimed, "all you gangsters get back in that hearse and clear outta hear. I got the woman hid where you'll never find her, so you just as well get on back to Detroit. Git, before I pull this trigger."

Gino came alive and took a step towards Guy. "What're you nuts?" he exclaimed, and threw both hands upward. "We just stopped to ask directions. What's with Detroit? We ain't from Detroit, we're from Chicago. And we ain't gangsters. We was sent here from the union to negotiate with the Clearwater Meat Company. So what's with the shotgun?"

Guy looked hesitant, then sheepish. "Well, why didn't you say so? When me and Emma saw the hearse and all, and you gents getting out all dressed up citylike, well, we just naturally thought . . ." Guy lowered the shotgun and Augie started breathing again.

Gino waved a finger at the others and all their hands reappeared from inside their coats.

Guy turned and called, "Come on out, Emma, and leave the shotgun. These gents are from the union. They want to see Abe."

He turned back to face Gino. "Wait a minute. What union?"

"The AFL-CIO Amalgamated Union. Big Ed sent a letter. We're supposed to get Clearwater Meat Company to join up."

Guy scratched his throat for a minute. "Can companies join the union? I thought only states could join the union, like Idaho."

Gino was lost. "What am I sayin' wrong? We're from the AFL-CIO and we was sent to negotiate with Clearwater Meat Company so they'd join the union. Is there somethin' about that you can't understand?"

"Well, no, when you say it that way," Guy allowed. "I just never knew companies could join a union. I thought only states."

Gino raised both hands, palms out. "Fergit it. Just tell us how to find Hollis."

"Yer in Hollis."

All seven men became zombies, and for ten full seconds the only sounds were the jays and squirrels in the trees and the gentle murmur of the river down the slope.

Finally Gino stammered, *"This is Hollis?"*

"Yeah, well, not all of it," Guy said defensively. "We got the church up there in them trees, and the school just behind it, and on down there's Ruby's bar and restaurant, and Wally's Repair Shop and some homes and stuff."

Gino licked dry lips and asked hesitantly, afraid of the answer. "Where's Clearwater Meat Company?"

"Three quarters of a mile on down the road. Can't miss it."

Gino looked pleading, nearly prayerful. "Is there a motel around here?"

Guy shook his head. "Nope. You figgerin' on stayin' a while?"

"The negotiations might take a week."

Emma said, "Well, there's folks here that got a spare room they'll rent. 'Course, you'll have to split up."

Gino shook his head violently. "Where's the nearest motel or hotel?"

Lewiston. That's twenty-eight—"

Gino cut in. "We know where Lewiston is." He took a deep breath and asked the next question as though he was resigned to death. "Is there a telephone around here?"

"Nope. Nearest phone's in—"

"Lewiston," Gino interrupted, and all the air left him. His shoulders slumped, and he stood with his head bowed in total defeat. Augie's eyes rolled back in his head. Vinnie winced. All the others turned their backs and muttered dark oaths under their breath.

Suddenly Gino raised his head, face white. "The mail! You got mail delivery out here?"

Guy looked offended. "Sure we get mail out here."

"Do you know if the Clearwater Meat Company got a letter lately?"

Guy pondered a moment. "Yeah, they did," he said, and suddenly a light went on in his head. "Was that from you guys?"

Gino exhaled in relief. "Yeah." He turned to face the others. "Okay, you guys, let's move it. We're two days late. We got to get on down to the negotiation. Get loaded."

Guy and Emma watched as the old hearse lurched back onto the gravelled road, groaned as it hit two pot-holes, hesitated when Augie shifted into second, and continued its weaving course, threading its way around the worst of the bumps and holes.

Guy shook his head. "Abe's in for the shock of his life. I wonder how he's goin' to take all this."

CHAPTER 4

"Who died?"

Beth stood stock-still inside the office, staring blank-faced at the hearse that had just eased off the road and parked in front of the plant.

"Haven't heard about nobody dyin'," Abe answered from the meat-cutting room.

"Did you call Peabody Mortuary?"

"Never heard of 'em," Abe said. He laid his knife scabbard on a cutting table and walked from the meat-cutting room into the office to stand beside her. His eyes popped.

Jack Durfee walked out of the boiler room. Jack was well over six feet tall, with a big, ruddy, moon face and a paunch. He could put an edge on a knife better than anyone else on the river, and while he looked like he was dawdling most of the time, he could bone meat and fix pickups faster than anyone within twenty miles. He had married Marge eight years ago, and usually showed up with one or two of his five kids when he came to work. Today he had come alone because Marge had two of them down with measles.

"Mattie satisfied?" he called as he walked through the meat-cutting room. They had finished working up Mattie's order half an hour ago, wrapped and loaded the fresh

44

sausage and pork chops and the head into apple boxes lined with newspapers, and put them in Mattie's pickup truck while Beth made the ledger entries. Puzzled at no response, Jack walked into the office to see Abe and Beth staring out the window like two statues. He bent over slightly to look out, to see what had frozen them.

"Well I declare," he said softly, "what is *that?*"

Outside, all the hearse doors opened at the same time and everyone got out. Gino, his face white and the tick twitching at the corner of his mouth, looked at the plant, then up and down the road, then across at Abe's house, then down at the river, then back at the plant. "May lightning strike me dead if that's the Clearwater Meat Company," he lamented.

Fearfully, Augie looked up at the clear sky.

Vinnie hunched forward and squinted. "The sign says it is." He pointed.

Inside, Beth swallowed and her voice croaked a little. "That must be part of the circus, the way they're dressed! I think I seen some posters they was comin' to Lewiston."

"The circus is Labor Day," Jack murmured. "I seen some guys like that in the Saturday morning matinee in Lewiston a while back, in the newsreel. They had tommy guns and hand grenades and the cops got 'em."

"I doubt they're from any mortuary," Abe concluded. He drew a deep breath and straightened. "I guess we better find out." He opened the office door and walked out, and Jack followed, while Beth stood in the doorway.

"Howdy, gents. What can I do for you?"

Gino walked over to Abe. "We're lookin' for the Clearwater Meat Company. That's a meat-packing plant

45

with a crew, and they do business. You know, a regular meatpacking company with big buildings and animals and stuff." He looked hopeful.

Abe scratched his chin. "This is it. You from Peabody Mortuary?"

Gino's eyebrows arched. "Do we look like a mortuary already?"

Abe pointed. "That's what the sign says on the hearse."

Gino's shoulders slumped as he remembered. "Sign, schmine! Signs don't mean nothin'. We're from the AFL-CIO Amalgamated Union. You get the letter from Big Ed?"

Abe thought for a moment. "Yeah. That you?"

"Big Ed's the boss. He sent us, like the letter said. Who're you?"

"Abe Jones. I own this plant. Me and Beth, my wife, in the doorway."

Gino glanced at Beth and tipped his hat. "Pleased to meetcha." He turned back to Abe. "Yeah, right. So where's your crew? I'm supposed to start with your crew."

Abe jabbed a thumb towards Jack. "That's him."

Gino's mouth fell open for a moment. "You got one lousy guy on your crew?"

Jack jerked erect and thrust out his lower lip defiantly.

"Today, yeah," answered Abe. "And Jack ain't lousy."

Gino nodded to Jack. "No offense intended." He turned back to Abe. "So you got other guys works different days?"

"When they got time."

Gino looked hopeful. "Like, they don't work no forty hours regular a week?"

Abe shook his head. "Hardly ever."

Gino smiled broadly. "Yeah, right, well, so when do we talk to 'em?"

"About what?"

Gino's eyebrows peaked. "Like what ain't I sayin' right? About joinin' the union."

Abe shrugged. "Whenever you want, I guess. Beth can tell you where they all live."

Gino exhaled and slumped. "Somehow I ain't explainin' this right. See, what we do, we get 'em all together in one place, and we talk to 'em all at the same time. Just the crew. Not you owners. And we explain all about what a union can do for 'em. And then they vote, and they got a union." He reached inside his coat and instantly everybody except Vinnie shoved their right hands inside their coats. Gino pulled out a pamphlet and the others dropped their hands back to their sides.

"See," Gino said, "all this stuff is explained right here in this here brochure, which is published by the United States of America Department of Labor in Washington, D.C., so you'll know what you're supposed to do. I'm supposed to give this to you before we vote and you got a union."

Abe took the pamphlet and slipped it in the bib pocket of his overalls. "Thanks. I'll study it."

Gino shook his head. "No, you ain't got the idee yet. You're supposed to study it *now* and I'm supposed to hold the first organizin' meetin' tomorrow. So where you got a room big enough for the meetin'?"

"You could use the meat-cutting room."

47

"Right. Got tables and chairs?"

"No."

"We can't have no meetin' without no table and chairs. Where you got some tables and chairs?"

Abe scratched his neck. "The school, or the church."

"Right. So what you gotta do, you gotta get all your guys in one room, and I gotta sit down with 'em at tables and chairs, and I gotta explain how Big Ed's union can help 'em. And then we gotta vote. Simple, see? Take maybe twenny minutes. Then I head back to Chicago and you're a union company. Nothin' to it."

Abe shrugged. "I suppose Beth can have 'em at the church by tomorrow afternoon." He looked at her and she nodded.

"Good. Great. See, nothin' to it. You get 'em here, I talk to 'em at four o'clock, we vote, I'm outta here at four-thirty, it's over, you got your union. Okay?"

Abe pondered for a moment. "What if they vote no?"

Gino thrust his face forward. "So what's to vote no? They ain't gonna vote no."

"But if they do, what then?"

"It's right there in that pamphlet I gave you. What happens then is, you got to get a United States of America genuine certified mediator in here, and he sits down with both sides and he explains everything to 'em, and they negotiate, and then they settle all their differences, and then they vote yes, and they got a union. See? So either way, they get a union. Ain't no sense in gettin' no mediator, because it all comes out the same anyway. I done this a hunnerd times. Trust me."

Abe rounded his lips and blew air. "Well, okay, if that's what's supposed to happen, we'll put out the word. Four o'clock tomorrow."

"Right. Oh, I almost forgot. We gotta look at your business books before so we'll know who your guys are and the number of hours they work, and stuff like that."

"You want Beth's ledger?"

"So what's with Beth's ledger? We want the reg'lar books in which you keep all your figgers showing how much business you done, how much you paid your crew, how much you paid for supplies and stuff, and how much profit you made, stuff like that. That's why we brung Vinnie, over there with the glasses. He knows numbers. That's the rules. You got to show us those books."

"The books are Beth's ledger."

"One ledger?"

Abe shrugged. "Only got one business."

"Yeah, okay, fine. We need that ledger now so we can look it over tonight."

Abe's face clouded. "It wouldn't be seemly to let the ledger get out of the office. You be here an hour early tomorrow and we'll let you study it."

Gino bristled. "That ain't the rules. Like I told you, you got to let us see those records."

"And I said okay, for an hour tomorrow, with Beth watchin'." Abe set his jaw.

Vinnie coughed. "An hour tomorrow is okay," he said quietly to Gino.

"Yeah all right, so we come an hour early. You have the ledger up at the church."

"Okay. If that guy reads records, what do the rest of your guys do?" Abe studied Augie and the others.

"Uh, well, like, those are, uh, . . . specialists. Yeah. That's right. Specialists."

"At what?"

"Explainin'." Gino grinned triumphantly. "Now, where's the church?"

"Back yonder, this side of Feeney's. Up from the road. Can't miss it."

"You miss the appointment," Gino said to Abe, "they send in a federal mediator. Federal means U.S. Government. You want the U.S. Government comin' down on you?"

"We'll be there."

Gino turned to Abe. "Nice meetin' you," he said perfunctorily. "Nice meetin' you too, ma'am." He tipped his hat to Beth, then led his men back to the hearse and they all piled in. Abe and Beth and Jack silently watched the hearse settle clear to the shocks and heard it groan as it labored back up the slight incline to the road and headed back toward Lewiston.

Beth pursed her mouth. "I've got a bad feeling about this."

Jack silently shook his head and started for his pickup.

"Jack," Beth called after him, "you stop and tell Al, and tell him to tell Elbert. Tomorrow at four o'clock at the church. I'll get the others."

At four o'clock the following afternoon the church was jammed to the walls. Word had gotten out. There's goin' to be a union meeting at old Fry's church, and the union men travel in a hearse filled with dead bodies, and they wear green suits and hats like outta the newsreels.

Too late the Hollis Unitarian Church minister, Oscar Fry, realized he'd missed his chance to make a small fortune. At two bits a head he'd have cleared nearly ten dollars, more than he'd seen in the plate on Sunday last month.

At 4:02 P.M. Fry walked out the little door behind the choir benches and marched to the pulpit.

Oscar Fry had graduated from the sixth grade fifty-eight years earlier, and had never been back to any school, least of all a seminary. Six years in the coal mines and on a tramp steamer convinced him his future was in something less strenuous, so he spent two years riding the rails between hobo camps, hitting every tent or open air revival meeting he could find. Between meetings he climbed into an empty boxcar and practiced thrusting his finger and shouting sermons like he'd seen the preachers at the revival meetings. Once he got it all perfected, he declared himself a born-again minister and went looking for his ministry. Too many people in Lewiston knew their Bible, so he moved up the river. He ran out of money at Feeney's, suddenly received revelation from on high, and declared the Spirit had led him to this humble settlement to serve the good, upright Christians.

He got the square, plain church built, but that's as far as the money and the charity of his flock would go, so he built a new bench every time he got another two dollars he could spare. Over twenty-eight years he had gathered enough benches, a raised pulpit, choir benches behind, and a big pine table for the sacraments.

The Reverend Fry was average height, gaunt, looked severe most of the time, and usually spoke too loud because he was a little hard-of-hearing. He thought his great thatch of white hair made him look like Moses, and he practiced a lot at carrying his Bible like he imagined Moses carried the stone tablets down from the mountain. And, whatever his shortcomings, he worked hard, was always there for sickness among his flock, lived frugally and mostly by the sweat of his own toil, helped build on an extra room at homes when babies arrived, walked to visit everyone in his parish twice a year, and was only found drunk once—down in the church basement amid six empty sacramental wine bottles.

He stood at the pulpit and cleared his throat, and the buzzing stopped.

"Dear children," he said in a loud voice. "We are gathered here this afternoon for the purpose of talkin' about a union. Not the union that binds together our great forty-eight states." He paused. "Not the ordained union by which a man and a woman enter into matrimony." He thrust his finger upward, arms length. "But the AFL-CIO union, by which these gents down here on my left has come into our fold to get the meat plant to join!"

He reared back and thrust out his chin. His lower lip protruded slightly and there was lightning in his eyes. He leaned forward and continued.

"A union is sacred and holy. The promises made cannot be broken without terrible consequences. A plague of frogs! The river turned to blood! Like Moses, in the Letter to the Galatians. So you must *humble* yourselves!" His finger punched a hole in the air. "You must seek divine power! I can feel 'er comin' right now! Can you?"

Nobody spoke.

He roared "*Can you?*"

"*Hallelujah, I can feel it!*" It surged from nearly everyone in the church excepting Gino and his men. They sat behind the sacramental table, faces turned to Oscar, eyes wide, fixed, every muscle in their bodies locked as though in a trance.

Oscar paused and studied his flock. Then he looked down into the stunned faces of Gino and the others at the sacramental table. He drew a breath while he considered whether or not he had met his duty to his flock. Yep, by any fair estimate he had prepared everybody for the AFL-CIO union, whatever that was.

He looked again at his flock. Charlie and Evelyn were sitting on the first bench, right smack in front of him, and instantly he searched his mind for what day of the month this was. The nineteenth! He flared his nostrils and inhaled slightly for confirmation, and there was doubt. He silently thanked the powers that be that it wasn't the thirtieth.

"So I now invite you to enter into Christian discussions with our welcome guests. I yield the pulpit to Mr. Gino."

He retreated to the corner chair reserved for the choir director, sat down, and looked expectantly at Gino.

Vinnie jabbed Gino in the ribs. "I think you're supposed to do something."

Gino jumped. "Huh?" He shook his head, made the mental journey back from where Oscar had taken him, and slowly got his bearings. He walked to the pulpit and faced the church.

Everywhere he looked there were people. Men with women beside them, children in their laps or seated next to them, faces half hidden behind mama's or daddy's arm as they peered at the pulpit. The facial expressions were identical. Mostly a deep curiosity, with a little fear and puzzlement mixed in. Gino took a deep breath to begin—and froze. His nose wrinkled and his eyebrows peaked. He looked down behind the pulpit, then back at the choir benches, and could see nothing. He again faced the crowd.

"See, it's like his Reverence said, this here is a meetin' to organize a union. I'm Gino Ponzi, and over here at this table is Vinnie, and Augie, and my specialists. We was sent here to explain how unions works, so you can vote and get your own union."

A wayward breeze drifted in from the open back doors, past Evelyn, into Gino's face, and again he froze for a moment, then continued.

"So the rules is, I'm supposed to talk with the employees that works for the meat plant. All except Abe and Beth Jones, who can't attend because they're the owners. See, them's the rules. Okay?"

Again his nose wrinkled, and he turned and took two quick paces to Oscar. "You got somethin' dead up around that pulpit?"

Oscar shook his head and quietly whispered. "That's Evelyn, right there in the front row."

Gino's eyes bugged for a second, and he returned to the pulpit.

"Okay, so I wantcha to meet my specialists." He walked quickly from the pulpit, over to the sacramental table. "This here's Vinnie and Augie, like I said. And here we got Dom and Franco and Guiseppe and Tony."

He stayed in front of the table. "So like I said, we're supposed to talk with the employees of the meat plant, but nobody else. Which means that whilst we appreciate all you others comin', you gotta leave."

Nobody moved.

"Um, them's the rules of the United States Department of Labor in Washington, D.C. Like Oscar said, unions is supported by heaven. So all you good people are supposed to leave."

Murmuring broke out.

"Is there somethin' secret about this?" Marge asked. "Secret things are usually not good."

"No, oh no, absolutely not," Gino said. "Nothin' like that. It's just the rules." He hunched forward to peer closely at one-year-old Danny, whom Marge was holding on her hip. "Er, lady, has that kid got a rash? Like, a disease maybe?"

Marge shrugged. "Measles."

Gino recoiled. "Shouldn't he be at home or in the hospital?"

"He's nearly over 'em. Won't hurt nobody."

Charlotte Fewkes stood. "My Jim works there a lot, and if the union has something to do with Abe's plant, it has something to do with all of us, because one way or another that business affects us all. So we got a right to hear this."

The clamor of affirmation crescendoed.

Gino looked at Vinnie, and Vinnie shrugged and nodded.

Gino threw up his hands and quieted the crowd. "Okay, okay, so you can stay. But the rules says, we got to get the crew up here to this table and them's the ones we talk to mainly. No talkin' by the rest of you. Okay?"

Grudging agreement came from the crowd.

"Okay, then, all you who work for the meat plant come on up here to the table."

Two minutes later, seven men had pulled chairs up to the sacramental table, facing Gino and his men.

"Okay. Now here's how we do it. I explain to you what the union can do for you, and then I ask you if you want to vote on getting the union, and then you vote. Everyone clear?"

Heads nodded.

"Okay. Vinnie's studied the books of the company and made a list. Vinnie, give me the list."

Vinnie produced several sheets of paper from his briefcase.

Gino grinned. "Okay. Here we go. Item 1. A guaranteed forty-hour week. How many hours a week you guys working right now?"

"Different hours."

"Okay, average. How many?"

"Oh maybe twenty-five, thirty."

"How would you like a guaranteed forty-hour week?"

"Can't give up that many hours. We got gardens and fishin' and huntin' to get set for winter."

"Okay, what about if you get paid for forty hours, and are still given time to do this other stuff?"

"You mean, get paid for forty hours every week, when we only work twenty-five?"

"Guaranteed." Gino looked triumphant.

The wives said, "That would be wonderful."

Gino bobbed his head. "Right. Next item. Guaranteed minimum wage, a buck and a quarter an hour. Vinnie says sometimes you get paid but not with money. True?"

"Yeah, it depends. Sometimes money, sometimes meat, sometimes usin' the smokehouse and other stuff."

"Want it all in hard cash? Buck and a quarter an hour, guaranteed?"

"You mean hard money every week?"

"Guaranteed."

"I ain't never seen that much money, regular."

"Right. Now yer gettin' the picture. Next item. Coffee breaks twice a day, once at 10 A.M. and once at 2:30 P.M. Ten minutes each."

"What do we do during them ten minutes?"

"You drink coffee."

Noses wrinkled. "Just sit around and drink coffee?"

"Yeah, right."

Shoulders shrugged.

"Next item. A regular dressing room. Where do you change your clothes now?"

"In the boiler room."

"That's out. Got to have a special dressing room and shower with lockers and stuff for each of you."

"Each with his own?"

"Guaranteed."

Heads shook in bewilderment.

"Next item. Time and a half for overtime."

"Come again?"

"Time and a half for overtime."

"What's overtime, and what's time and a half if it happens?"

"Overtime is any time over eight hours a day, and if you work past eight hours you get your buck and a quarter, plus an additional sixty-two cents each hour."

"Why? We don't do no more work than usual after the eight hours."

"Come on, wake up! Any slave driver pushes you past eight hours, he ought to pay you time and a half. You're worth it."

"What about we work ten hours one day and six the next?"

"Time and half for two hours, full time for fourteen."

Eyes widened.

"Next item. Fringe benefits. A pension. How would you like to retire in twenny years with enough money to live on the rest of your lives?"

Everybody leaned back in quiet disbelief. Elbert grinned. "You proposin' you can arrange that?"

"Guaranteed."

"How."

"Set up a union pension fund."

Elbert shook his head.

"Next item. Health plan. You got a kid with the measles, you get a doctor. Your wife has another kid, you get a doctor."

Nobody was moving anymore. Their minds had long since gone into paralysis.

"Then there's worker's compensation. You get hurt on the job, you get paid until you're able to work again.

And there's guaranteed holiday, and you get off with pay on your birthday, and you get paid leave when your kids is born."

Gino paused and looked up from the list and for a moment wondered at the thousand-yard stare in every eye. Not even the children moved.

"Next item. If you're a specialist in somethin', you get journeyman's pay. Journeyman beef skinners, three bucks ten cents an hour. Headers, two bucks and four bits an hour. Shrouders, two bucks an hour. Breakers, two bucks ten cents an hour. Sausage makers, two bucks ninety cents an hour. Eviscerators, minimum wage."

The soft, warm evening breeze could be heard. The faint murmur of the distant river filtered in. Gino stopped and looked across the table at the steady, dead eyes of the crew of the Clearwater Meat Company. Something inside whispered, "What they're hearin' ain't what you're sayin'."

He put his list down on the table. "Uh, this is what the union can do for you guys. You understand? Better wages, guaranteed hours, all them fringes and stuff, you understand?"

No one spoke.

"So what is it with you guys?"

Elbert cleared his throat and leaned forward. "You're saying your union can guarantee all them things for us guys who work for Abe and Beth?"

Gino brightened. "Guaranteed."

"In writing?"

"Guaranteed Union Contract."

"If we was to take this here guaranteed union contract over to the courthouse in Lewiston, would Judge Hoffstader say it was legal?"

"Guaranteed." Gino suddenly looked important. "But you wouldn't take that to the courthouse in Lewiston. You would take it to the United States District Court, because this here is important, and only them big United States judges handles these kinds of contracts."

"You guarantee all them things?"

"Absolutely."

Elbert turned to the rest of the crew and they turned their backs on Gino and huddled. "What do you think?"

Charlie shook his head. "He's dreamin'."

Al looked serious. "Won't hurt to see what she looks like. Get a copy of it."

"Jim?"

He shrugged. "Let's see what it says."

"Jack? Bill? Gene?"

"Let's take a look."

Elbert turned back to Gino. "Where do we get a copy of this contract? We'd like to take a look at her."

"Vinnie's got one right there." Gino looked grand while he waited for Vinnie to draw the four-page document out of his briefcase.

Elbert took it and again the crew huddled. At the end of the second paragraph they looked at each other in total bewilderment. Elbert blew air and shook his head. "Most of them words look like English, but I don't know nothin' about what I read."

He turned back to Gino. "A couple more things. How often does the union send all these checks to us, and why is the union doin' all this for us?"

Gino stopped cold and closed his eyes while his mind went back over Elbert's sentence. Suddenly it hit bottom and Gino shuddered.

"Hold on," he choked out. "What's this about the union sendin' checks?"

Elbert straightened. "All this forty hours business and time and a half, and pay when we don't work, and bein' paid while we're on vacation. You said the union guaranteed all that. When? When do you pay?"

Gino looked around the room. Fifty pair of mirthless, dead eyes impaled him. Women with kids on their hips, and others hanging on their skirts, didn't blink as their eyes bored holes in him. He felt sweat break out on his forehead.

Gino fished a handkerchief from his pocket and swabbed his face. "Er, look, maybe I said it wrong. See, what I meant was, you guys join the union, and the union makes the contract with the Clearwater Meat Company."

Elbert looked at Jim and Al and Jack for a moment, then back at Gino.

"But the union pays for all this stuff. Right? That's what you said. The union guaranteed it."

Gino froze. Vinnie bowed his head.

Elbert's eyes narrowed and he repeated himself. "Right? Like you guaranteed?"

"Well, yeah, right," Gino said, "only when we sign the contract with the meat company, they agree to pay it."

Insects could be heard buzzing one hundred yards away, through the open windows.

Elbert's face scrooched into a prune as he struggled to understand.

Finally he said, "Now hold on. You mean after we vote and get our union, then you go make Abe and Beth pay all the money and do all them things for us?"

Gino nodded vigorously and tried to control the tick in his face. "Well, like, yeah, that's how unions work. You join our union and we look out for you and do all kinds of good things."

"If you're talkin' straight, I must be listenin' crooked," Elbert observed. "I keep hearin' you say the union does all these good things for us, but Abe and Beth pays for it. If it's the union doin' it, how come it's Abe and Beth payin'?"

"They sign the union contract and that's what they agree to do."

"Abe and Beth ain't got the money to pay for all them good things, and if they ain't got the money, Abe ain't goin' to sign no union contract. And if Abe and Beth don't sign, then what happens?"

"Then we put on a union strike."

"Who's 'we', and what's a strike?"

Gino's eyes rolled up into his head for a second. "You guys who work for him don't go to work. If you don't go to work, then his business stops and that makes him sign. That's a union strike. We do it all the time."

Murmuring, and then open talk broke out.

Elbert said, "You mean we just up and don't go to work?"

"Yeah."

"Then how do we feed our women and kids?"

Gino swallowed. "Well, like, we pay you money from the union strike fund." He turned to Vinnie, new hope leaping in his eyes. "Right, Vinnie?"

"Yes." Vinnie nodded vigorously.

"You pay with union money?"

"Well, no not exactly," Gino began, and again turned to Vinnie, "you tell 'em Vinnie."

"That's paid out of the union strike fund."

"Then that's union money?"

Vinnie cleared his throat. "Well, no, that is, money from the union dues."

Elbert's head dropped forward and his eyes closed for a moment as he studied on it.

"Wait a minute," he said. "I can't hardly keep up with this. What's union dues?"

"Well," Gino said, "it's like, uh, . . ."

Elbert cut in. "Mr. Gino, would it be askin' too much to just cut out all the dumb stuff and get right to it? What's union dues?"

"That's the dues paid into the union by the members."

Elbert drew a deep breath. "Like taxes?"

Gino turned to Vinnie, pleading in his eyes.

Vinnie's voice cracked as he spoke. "Well, in a way, yes. If you belong to our union, part of your wages are paid to the union, so we can do all the things for you Gino has talked about."

"How much is the dues and how often?"

"Oh, usually about eight or ten dollars a month."

Gasps were heard all over the old church.

Quickly Vinnie added, "But that can be adjusted."

Elbert's face was a study in bewilderment as he pondered the whole scheme.

"How much money have we got in this union strike pot?"

"Well," Vinnie said hopefully, "that's a big bank account in Chicago, and right now there is a lot of money there because none of the unions have had to go on strike for quite a while."

"If we go on strike and use some of it, how does it get repaid?"

"An increase in union dues."

"If we just up and don't go to work, then how does Abe keep the plant goin'?"

Gino licked dry lips. "He can try to hire someone else, but if he tries to do that we send out pickets."

"What's pickets?"

"That's, uh, guys that go out there and walk around on the road with signs that says you're on strike because the employer—that's the meat plant— is unfair."

Elbert shook his head in total loss of understanding. "Wait a minute. You mean that me and Charlie and Al and the rest, we go down to Abe's meat plant and we walk up and down the road with signs that says Abe's a bum?"

"Not a bum," Gino blurted. "It says he's unfair to labor."

A crescendo of sound swamped the old church.

"Abe's unfair? You're tellin' us we'd have to carry signs sayin' Abe's unfair?"

"Well, yeah." The tick on Gino's face was going wild.

"Yer crazy!" Elbert blurted. "Abe and Beth's the most fair people on the river. They seen most of us through hard times and ain't never wavered. You think we're goin' down there and walk around like a bunch of idiots with signs that says Abe's unfair?"

"That's only if you have to go on strike."

Al tugged Elbert's sleeve and Elbert dropped his head down to listen for a minute, then straightened. "Mr. Gino, who pays you guys to do this? Who's your boss?"

Gino glanced at Vinnie, and Vinnie saw the beginnings of panic in his eyes. "Well, see, we work for the AFL-CIO."

Elbert was losing patience. "No more big talk. Who pays you? Who's your boss?"

Gino again turned to Vinnie.

"We are employed by the union. Big Ed is our president."

There was a long pause.

"And where does the union get the money to pay all you guys?"

Vinnie cleared his throat and swallowed, and fidgeted with his briefcase. The building became silent.

Elbert's eyes narrowed and his mouth puckered.

"From union dues," Vinnie said quietly.

Elbert's jaw dropped open. "One more time, and louder."

"From union dues."

An avalanche of sound swamped the building. Elbert turned to the rest of the crew and they huddled and things quieted, and still they talked with great animation and loud words, and finally Elbert turned back to Gino.

"I'm goin' to say this as straight as I can, considerin' you guys came in here and told it about as crooked as you could. You guys are sayin' that we vote for a union, and all those good things you said, and then you make us pay dues to the union, and then you make Abe and Beth sign to pay for all those good things, and if they don't sign, then we don't go to work, and we come down here and walk around with signs that says they're unfair. And if that don't work they try to hire someone else, or go broke. Yes or no. Have we got that right?"

Gino gathered up all the courage he could find, squared his shoulders, and looked directly at Elbert. "Yeah, well, look, that isn't exactly . . ."

Elbert had reached his limits. "Mr. Gino, not meanin' to be unfriendly, I'm goin' to ask you to kindly cut out the big city double-talk and give us a simple answer. Yes or no. I'll take one, or I'll take the other, but you go addin' your usual line of nonsense, and things will likely get active real quick."

Gino stared into Elbert's eyes for a split second and felt his heart flutter, and he said, "Yes."

Elbert again huddled with the crew for two minutes, then turned back to Gino.

"This here has got to be the genuine blue-ribbon, all-time meanest idee we ever heard of. You guys is nothin' but a bunch of mangy coyotes. You come in here with this big story of puttin' us all on easy street, but what you mean is, you make us pay you to wreck what Abe and Beth has spent forty years puttin' together and windin' up with no way of findin' work to feed our families. Meanwhile you guys are back in Chicago wearin' them dumb suits and drivin' hearses on union dues we paid. I ain't sure how you figgered to blow all this past us, but you might be a whole lot happier if you went somewhere else with this union stuff, because your health might do some sufferin' if you stay around here with it."

Elbert turned on his heel and marched out the back of the church. Al followed, the rest of the crew right behind. Then the women and kids and neighbors looked at Gino the way they looked at rattlesnakes and followed the men.

Evelyn was the last to rise. Before she left, she walked up to Gino, toe to toe, face to face, her nose wrinkled in disgust.

Gino caught and held his breath.

"Abe and Beth's meat plant's the only place my Charlie has got work since he was gassed in World War I. And you want us to pay you to ruin it?"

Gino was turning blue.

Evelyn continued. "Ain't much worse things I can think of than robbin' a cripple of the only job he can get."

Gino's eyes were bugging out. His neck veins were protruding. His face was turning black. Franco looked at him, alarmed, and turned to Dom. "Lookit Gino! I think he's dyin'."

Slowly Evelyn turned and walked down the aisle. When she cleared the back door, Gino grabbed the table to keep from falling and exhaled explosively and gasped great draughts of air. Slowly his eyes settled back into his sockets, and the color began to come back to his face.

Oscar slowly walked over to him. "Come in here friendly like, and then do what you done." He shook his head sadly. "There was this fella in the Bible named

Judas. He acted friendly too, and then he sold his friend for money. You might want to read about it. Book of Genesis."

CHAPTER 5

"Number pleeuzz."

Alice Beesley sat at the big Lewiston switchboard, headset clamped on, hand poised with the plug to complete the connection.

Alice was plump, compulsively fussy, and wore her hair piled on top of her head with hairpins sticking out. She had her high school diploma framed on the wall above her switchboard. No one in central Idaho knew more about the current state of gossip than Alice, because her switchboard was the crossroads for everything. Contrary to the rules, she seldom missed listening to private calls, and party lines were her specialty. When three or four of the locals got into a party line gossip session, Alice unabashedly jumped smack in the middle, and was a welcome addition because of all the juicy stuff she'd heard in the last day or two. It made the telephone gossip game a study in revealing sworn secrets and waiting a couple of days to see how far they had spread.

On those occasions when Buster's voice came onto the line, Alice's face would flush and her heart would flutter as she stammered and then invented ways to carry on with him without him ever knowing she loved him forever. In the late evenings she would often sit in the swing on the front porch of the boardinghouse and gaze at the moon while she trembled at the remembrance of that moment of moments in her life when Buster had whopped her in the stomach after the marble game and won her heart forever.

"Yeah, operator? I gotta place a person-to-person long-distance call to Big Ed in Chicago."

Alice's eyebrows arched. A long-distance call from Lewiston to Chicago at 7:30 A.M.? "Chicago?" she asked.

"Yeah. Chicago. Like in windy and Lake Michigan? Chicago, you know?"

Alice frowned. "What is the Chicago number?"

"It's, uh—Vinnie, what's that number?—yeah, 6628. Person-to-person to Big Ed."

"Hold, pleeuzz." Alice worked the plugs and listened. "Your number is ringing." She drove the last plug home and left the key open. Why would someone in the Lumberjack hotel be calling Chicago?

On the third ring the nasal, high voice came piercing. "Yeah, union here, Irene speakin'. With whom do you wish to speak with?"

"Get Big Ed on."

Irene leaned back and yelled, "Eddy Baby, Gino's on the line."

Gino heard Big Ed's phone click open. "Yeah, Big Ed here. Tell me you got a new chapter of the union out there."

"Yeah, well, close but not exactly. See, we had our first meetin' yesterday afternoon."

Big Ed chopped him off. "You didn't get no new chapter?"

"Naw, we, uh, well, we're goin' to have to talk with these guys a little longer."

Big Ed jerked the cold cigar out of his mouth and sat bolt upright. "What happened?"

Gino shrugged. "These rednecks don't know from nothin'. See, they thought the union was supposed to pay all the overtime and vacations and pension and stuff."

Alice's jaw thrust out. Rednecks! Who's a redneck? What's a redneck?

"Awww," Big Ed groaned, "Gino, you stupid or somethin'? You didn't explain it right."

"I done it like always, but Boss, you gotta understand, this bunch is like pilgrims, like they just got off the Mayflower."

Alice's mouth became firm.

"Where did you meet?"

"In a church."

"Who was there?"

"The whole lousy countryside. Men, women, kids— the whole bunch."

Alice's nose wrinkled. Lousy!

"You ran the meeting?"

"Yeah. Well, not the first part."

"Who did that?"

"The preacher."

"What did he say?"

"That unions was like sacred and holy, like the union when you get married, and the union of the forty-eight states."

Big Ed's face wrinkled in bewilderment. "He said *what*?"

"Look, Boss, like I ain't never seen nothin' like this before. Gimme a couple days and we'll have this thing

71

iced. We'll just have to talk a little more and they'll be fine."

"Gino, you listen to me good! You make somethin' happen so we can yell foul and get an unfair labor practice charge goin'. You understand that?"

"Yeah, right, Boss, oh sure, right. I'll do that."

Big Ed jammed the cigar back in the corner of his mouth. "You can't handle this, you say so. I'll send out somebody who can."

"Now, Boss, you just leave it to me. I'll ice this in two days. I'll call."

"Meeting in a church, a crazy preacher, union of states! Gino, you been drinkin' already this mornin'?"

"Boss! You have injured me. Honest, I ain't had nothin' to drink since I got here."

"You been in a bus wreck or somethin'?"

"What bus? Oh, yeah, the bus. Naw, the road was out, so we couldn't take the bus. We come in a . . . vehicle."

There was another pause. "Gino, what ain't you tellin' me? What kind of vehicle?"

"Uh, well, it was . . . see, we didn't have no choice. We come up in a hearse."

Big Ed lunged forward and half rose out of his chair. "A *what?*"

"Look, Boss, yer gonna have to trust me. There wasn't no other way. Just give me two more days. I promise, we'll fix this thing up and you'll have the whole state of Idaho within two weeks. Honest. Trust me."

Big Ed stood bolt upright. "You got two days. You can't handle that bunch of pencil-necks, I'll get someone who can."

Alice's eyes popped. Pencil-necks!

"I can do it, Boss, I can. Two more days."

"You got forty-eight hours."

The phone clicked dead.

Alice pulled the plugs and sat back in her chair. She stored every word of Gino's conversation in her memory while she worked with the plugs, handling the early-morning calls.

Alice Beesley could quote more than three thousand conversations by heart, from the hottest, best, juiciest telephone calls in central Idaho from 1942 on. She knew the makings of sensational gossip when she heard it, and she had just heard it. She didn't yet know how the Chicago conversation was going to stir things up, but nothing was more certain than the fact that it would. Her eyes glowed with sweet anticipation as she took the next plug and mechanically repeated, "Number pleeuzz."

•₀ ○ ○ •₀

Vinnie looked at Gino, who swabbed sweat from his white face with a handkerchief while the nervous tick started. "Big Ed is upset?"

Gino avoided the question. "We got to get finished in two days, or else."

"How?"

"We got to figger a way to get an unfair labor practice charge goin'. That's how."

Augie said, "That I can do." He smiled eagerly and reached inside his coat.

"Naw," Gino said, "you keep the artillery hid. We ain't down to that yet. Let me think." He began to pace while he rubbed his chin.

Dom spoke up. "Uh, maybe we could just kidnap . . ." Dom started.

Gino thrust his finger in the air. "Ah-ha! Got it. We go out there and wait for one of the crew to deliver some meat or somethin' to one of them families up there, and we stop the truck real friendly and ask 'em what they got, and we go through it and maybe happen to accidentally break open a package or two of meat, and that makes 'em mad, so they start somethin' and we got 'em."

"Yeah," Augie said, "good thinkin'."

"Get loaded!" Gino exclaimed, "and bring the artillery. We're headed right back out there to get us an unfair labor practice."

•• ○ ○ •• ○

Twenty-eight miles east, in the clear, sparkling air of a Rocky Mountain morning, Elbert eased his pickup down close to the door of the meat plant and waved at Charlie, who was just getting in his pickup to leave.

"Howdy," Elbert called. "Headed somewhere special?"

Charlie grinned his tired, sad grin and said, "Yeah, Abe asked me to take them hams and smoked fish on down to Kenny Eubanks's place. Kenny's fixin' the brakes on his pickup."

Elbert nodded, and Charlie cranked up his battered old truck, ground the gears into low, and pulled out. Elbert walked into the office.

"Mornin'," Abe said. "Charlie was tellin' me what happened yesterday."

"Yeah!" Elbert exclaimed, "them guys is crazy. I still can't get hold of how they come in here like they done,

makin' all them promises and never told us they fig-
ered to make you pay for 'em."

Three quarters of a mile west, Guy Feeney paused
and walked out of his store at the sound of a six-cylinder
1936 Chevy with a rod clattering and the gearbox grinding, and waved at Charlie as he passed. A mile and a half
later Charlie slowed fifty yards before he came to the
potholed dirt lane to the Eubanks's place, when he saw
the oncoming vehicle. It startled him so bad that he
threw on the brakes, and the two right wheels locked as
usual and spun the pickup to a stop nearly sideways in
the road. Charlie shifted down and straightened the
pickup in the road, then leaned forward to gape.

Suddenly he reared back. "Oh man, it's them union
guys in that hearse," he said. He pondered a moment. "I
better get this meat up to Kenny and then head back to
warn Abe." He jammed the clutch to the floor, jerked
the gearshift down and to the left, and let the clutch out.
The pickup lurched forward, and Charlie started to make
the right turn.

The hearse shifted over and stopped smack dab in
front of him, radiator cap to radiator cap. Charlie
jammed on the brakes, swallowed, and sat frozen to the
wheel. The hearse emptied, and all seven men casually
sauntered down to surround Charlie and his truck.

"Just a neighborly visit," Gino said, and looked at the
cardboard boxes with Sego Milk printed on the side, sitting in the pickup bed with wrapped meat packages.
"Makin' a delivery?"

"Nuh-nuh-nuh no," Charlie stammered, "Abe just
asked me to drop this off at the Eubanks on the way
home."

"Yeah, well, that's right neighborly, ain't it. Nice of you to let us take a look at them packages."

"Uh, that ain't my meat," Charlie said. "You oughtn't mess around with it."

"Just lookin'," Gino said, and Dom and Franco reached to flip the packages out of the first box. They tore the paper wrap nearly off the hams.

"Hey," Gino scolded. "Be careful with them packages. That meat belongs to . . ." he turned back to Charlie. "Who does that belong to?"

"Kenny Eubanks."

"Yeah, right," Gino said, smiling. "That meat belongs to Kenny Eubanks. Be careful with it."

"Yeah, right," Augie said, and he grinned as he tipped the second box over.

Charlie sighed and got out of the pickup. "Don't do that no more," he said, and he straightened the boxes and rolled the hams back inside the paper as best he could and laid them back in the boxes.

"Right," Franco said, and tipped them both over as soon as Charlie had finished.

Charlie's face dropped forward and he stepped back while they tore the paper off the hams.

"I told you guys," Gino exclaimed, "don't damage the meat."

"Oh," Dom said. "We done a mistake. Clumsy, I guess." Franco laughed out loud.

Gino gave a head nod and the others went back to the hearse.

"Like, you gotta overlook those guys," he said. "They didn't mean no harm. Just clumsy. Nice talkin' to yuh."

Gino swaggered back to the hearse. Charlie got into his pickup, turned it around, and headed back to the meat plant. The sound of the clattering rod brought Abe's head up, and Elbert walked out the office door.

"Somethin' wrong up at Eubanks?" Elbert called.

Charlie got out and shook his head. "No, I got to rewrap the meat."

"Had an accident?"

"Nope. Them union guys."

Elbert's jaw dropped open. "What happened?"

"They stopped me up there past Feeney's and messed up the meat."

Abe walked to the truck and looked. "Nothin' serious. Won't take five minutes. Give me a hand, Elbert."

Five minutes later Elbert turned to Abe, his face a blank, his voice low and easy. "I'll take this stuff to Kenny."

Abe took a deep breath. "Better let me. They get you peeved, things could happen. We don't want no trouble."

Elbert picked up a box and started for his pickup. "Won't be no trouble unless they start it."

Abe watched Elbert's pickup disappear going west, and three minutes later Guy watched Elbert's pickup rattle past his store. Guy scratched his scraggly four-day growth of whiskers for a minute. "Charlie went west and come back, and now there's Elbert, doin' the same thing." Guy suddenly jerked erect.

"Emma, come a-runnin'," he hollered. "If I got this figgered right, we're about to see some fireworks like we ain't seen in a long time. Leave the front door open in case someone needs somethin' while we're gone, and get in the truck!" A minute later he was dodging potholes as he headed west, in Elbert's dust, Emma grim-faced beside him with both arms braced against the dented dashboard.

Elbert slowed at the Eubanks's lane and looked up the road. Suddenly the black hearse appeared from behind a big growth of scrub oak and brush. Elbert stopped and the hearse stopped, nose to nose with the pickup. Elbert got out and the hearse emptied.

A quarter-mile back, Guy stepped on the brakes and slid his truck to a stop. "This is far enough," he said to Emma. "I don't want to be no part of what's goin' to happen up there if they get Elbert peeved. We'll watch from here."

Elbert walked towards Gino. "Can I help you gents with somethin'?"

"Yeah, well, this is just a social call," Gino said. "Just out drivin' and seen you and figgered we ought to stop and pay our respects."

"Well, you done that, so I guess I'll be movin' on," Elbert said. "I got some stuff to deliver up there to Kenny and Zelda."

"Oh well now, is that a fact?" Augie said. "Makin' a delivery for the meat plant?"

Elbert shrugged. "I guess so. Abe asked me to do it."

"What you got?" Gino said. The others surrounded the truck and Dom and Franco reached for the boxes and began roughing up the packages.

"Hey!" Elbert exclaimed. "That there's Kenny's meat. You guys ought not be doin' that."

Dom reached into the first box and ripped open one package.

Gino grinned. "Clumsy. Just clumsy."

"Well, you fellas just get away from there," Elbert said.

Augie tipped over the other box and tore open a package.

Elbert said, "Charlie told me what you done to him. Now I'm tellin' you, cut that out. I'm gettin' just a little peeved."

Dom grinned. "Careless of us."

Gino shrugged. "They're just playful. No harm."

"Now, that's enough," Elbert said. "You get on away from there."

Dom reached for Elbert, and that's the last thing Dom remembered that bright June morning, until about four o'clock in the afternoon. Elbert's fist caught him flush on the point of his chin and Dom went down flat on his back in the dusty road, with arms and legs thrown wide, his face as peaceful as that of a baby.

For two seconds the other six stared down at Dom, dumbstruck, and then Franco and Augie came up on both sides of Elbert. Augie's eyes were big, his face flushed. "Look what you done to Dom!" he exclaimed.

"You just back off and this'll stop right here," Elbert said.

Augie and Franco each reached for one of Elbert's arms, and four seconds later they had joined Dom, flat on their backs, breathing deep with the innocent expression of angels on their slack faces.

Elbert turned to the four still standing. "I'm gettin' a little peeved, and I'm about to lose my temper. If any of you got ideas like these three, why, just speak up right now and we'll finish this. If you don't, then grab one of these guys and help me load 'em into your outfit."

Gino was standing like a statue. So was Tony.

Guiseppe swallowed and tried to say something, but his voice wouldn't work.

Elbert pointed to Tony. "Grab that first guy and get him into that outfit. I'll bring the others."

Tony grabbed Dom under the arms and dragged him to the back door of the hearse while Elbert grabbed the others by the backs of their coat collars and a minute later piled them into the hearse. He turned to Gino.

"You best get on back wherever you came. We don't take kindly to you scarin' Charlie and messin' with Kenny's hams and bacon. Now git."

Elbert started back to the door of his pickup.

Guiseppe pulled his .45 automatic from inside his coat.

Vinnie fainted dead away in a heap.

Gino yelled, "Guiseppe, hold on. Big Ed said no shootin'."

Elbert dived inside the cab of his truck and grabbed his twelve-gauge Remington shotgun from the rack in the back window. Elbert always figured the law that required shotgun magazines to be plugged to allow just two shells was a dumb law, and he had long since pulled the plug out of the Remington magazine. He kept it loaded with seven shells, double-ought buckshot loads, for geese.

He whipped the muzzle of the Remington towards the hearse, where Guiseppe was partially hidden by the open door. Guiseppe raised his pistol, and Elbert touched off the first roaring blast from the twelve-gauge. The buckshot blew the glass completely out of the door beside Guiseppe. Guiseppe jumped about a foot in the air and hit the ground running away from the ruined door. Elbert tracked him with the muzzle of the shotgun and Guiseppe stopped.

"Now you gone and done it," Elbert hollered. "You got me peeved. You throw down that pistol and you get all the guns from these other guys and pile 'em together right out there in the road, and then you load up and get outta here."

Guiseppe nodded his head eight times in two seconds, threw his pistol down like it was a scorpion, and thirty seconds later had fourteen pistols and two tommy guns in a pile in the middle of the road.

"Now you get in that contraption and you get outta here and don't come back," Elbert yelled.

Guiseppe nodded briskly and leaped behind the wheel. He revved up the engine to about 4,000 rpms and popped the clutch, and the old Packard transmission whined as it spun the wheels and threw dirt fifty feet, while it left trenches four inches deep in the country road. The hearse ripped backwards forty yards before Guiseppe could stop it and turn around, and he left, travelling west at racing speed, heedless of the potholes that were bouncing it all over the road.

Elbert watched them until they cleared the last rise in the road three minutes later, four miles west, then he put the Remington back in the window rack. He got a piece of hay-baling wire from the back of his pickup, walked to the guns piled in the road, slipped it through the trigger guards and wired them together, then dumped them in the bed of the pickup. He straightened out Kenny's meat the best he could and drove on to Kenny's place.

"Thought I heard a shotgun," Kenny said as Elbert put the last box on the porch. Zelda was in the doorway, the ten-month-old on her hip, the two-year-old hanging on her skirt.

"Yeah," Elbert said, "that was me. Some of them union guys showed up. They messed up some of your meat packages."

"Anyone get hurt?" Zelda asked.

"Nope."

Kenny said, "Someone had an engine wound up pretty tight."

Elbert shrugged. "That was them, leavin'."

Kenny puckered his forehead. "Think they're gone for good and all?"

"I doubt it. Likely they'll be back." Elbert reflected for a minute. "We'll wait and see."

CHAPTER 6

Lewiston, Idaho, came into being because of Meriwether Lewis and William Clark. Meriwether Lewis was the private secretary to President Thomas Jefferson in 1804. Jefferson had just bought the Louisiana Territory from the French, because it was cheaper to buy it than to go to war and steal it. However, once he owned it Jefferson got bored, because he couldn't find a war to start, or anything really big to buy, like another territory, and soon he became grumpy. One grumpy day he happened to look at his big wall map and suddenly wondered what was out west of the Louisiana Territory, and whether it was worth owning.

He called in his secretary, Meriwether. "Meri, go find someone in Congress that lives out there in Louisiana and ask them what kind of land they got west of them, and who owns it."

Next morning Meriwether reported. "No one really knows."

Jefferson frowned and said, "Meri, I got to know what's out there. Who can we get to go find out?"

"Me," Meri said. "I've been a soldier and been out on bivouacs before, and I got this drinking buddy named Bill Clark down at Mulrooney's Tavern. He draws good maps and pictures of animals and birds and stuff. Him and me can go out there for a couple of weeks and draw up some maps and birds and animals, and you can see for yourself."

"Hah!" Jefferson exulted. "Get him in here."

So the next Saturday night after Meri and Bill left Mulrooney's, they dropped by the White House. Jefferson asked them in for a nightcap or two, and about two o'clock in the morning Jefferson said, "Meri, you and Bill got the job. Get on out there west of Louisiana and make a map and draw some things. Find out who owns it, and if they're fighters or not, so we'll know how big an army we'll need to go take it away from 'em."

And Meri and Bill did it.

Sometime in 1805 they hit Clearwater River. It was nestled in some mountains and plains, with a lot of forests, and was beautiful, and they figured it would be a nice place for a town, so they staked out a townsite. They had to cross the river to continue west, so Bill crossed the Clearwater first, and when he got to the other side he hollered back to Meri, "Hey, there's a better place for a town right over here."

Meri hollered back: "Can't be. The town oughta be right here where we staked it out."

They argued for about twenty minutes, hollering back and forth across the Clearwater, so finally Meri hollered: "Tell you what, Bill. You go right ahead and set a townsite over there for yourself, and I'll keep this one over here on this side for me."

And they did.

Today, Lewiston, Idaho, has grown on the east side of the Clearwater, and Clarkston, Washington, on the west side.

With western white pine so thick the mountains look like a green carpet, and the Clearwater River there to carry logs, lumberjacks swarmed in, and with them came their habits and mind-set. They were tough and loud and rowdy, and they scoffed at the refinements of life east of the Mississippi, and at the government in Washington, D.C. They ate about anything the camp cooks could get into the ovens or over a roasting fire, slept in tents, bathed every Saturday night before they went to the nearest tavern, and boasted they could wrestle grizzly bears. And some of them could, and a few of them did.

By the close of World War II, Lewiston had blossomed into a respectable little town with a lumber mill on the banks of the Clearwater, but the basic notions of the founding fathers lingered on. Lewiston still had little patience with ideas from east of the Mississippi, and they considered all the politicians in Washington, D.C., in the same genre as rattlesnakes, with some apologies to the snakes.

Back in 1886, Lewiston boasted one hotel, the Lumberjack, built of unpeeled logs. It was square and austere, with two stories, one washroom for ten rooms, and a four-holer outhouse in back. By 1947 the sole improvements to the Lumberjack hotel were electricity, a telephone for the clerk, a pay telephone by the front door for the public, and indoor plumbing. They had an electric lightbulb on a dropcord in each room and one toilet on the main floor, a circumstance that required considerable planning by all guests and some heavy refereeing by the hotel clerk.

By that time there was a motel in town, named the Aloha. It got that name because someone heard Lowell Thomas say "Aloha" in the newsreel of a Saturday night picture show at the Roxy theatre and thought it was mysterious and entrancing, and it didn't have anything to do with snooty eastern attitudes or Washington, D.C. So they built the motel and got a genuine neon sign that said "Aloha" and had a girl with a grass skirt, and the grass skirt switched back and forth when the girl did.

The first night they turned on the sign, Chigger Tubbs came driving his twenty-six-wheeler logging truck through town with a full load of about fifteen tons of logs chained down. He drove past the motel, saw the grass skirt switching, and his eyes bugged half out of his head. He froze at the wheel and ran over two parked pickups, one Ford, the other a Chevy, before he came back to his senses and rassled the truck to a stop. They had to arrest him, and he went to trial, and the jury decided he wasn't guilty. Why, anybody would of got in a wreck, first time they saw that sign with that grass skirt switchin' back and forth, and all. For the next two weeks Clyde had two deputies in front of the Aloha directing traffic while Lewiston got used to a hula girl with a switching grass skirt.

Two weeks before Augie and the hearse drove in, a fire burned part of the Aloha, and it was closed for repairs, but about ready to open one wing. However, that one wing didn't have enough rooms for everybody Big Ed had sent, so Augie and the others were lodged in three rooms on the second floor of the Lumberjack.

Such was the state of affairs on the glorious June morning when Gino picked the earpiece off the public pay telephone in the lobby of the Lumberjack to tell Big Ed about their battle with Elbert on the previous day. He dropped his nickel clinking into the slot, and waited.

"Number pleeuzz."

"Yeah, person-to-person, collect to Chicago, for Big Ed. The number is . . ."

"6628," Alice said, and Gino's eyebrows raised as she drove the plugs home. Circuits closed and Alice said, "Your party is on the line," and she settled in, eyes wide, eyebrows raised.

"Hey, Big Ed," said Gino excitedly, "we done it. We got us an unfair labor charge."

Alice's eyebrows arched in surprise.

Big Ed said, "What happened?"

"Boss," Gino crowed, "it was beautiful. There was about twenty of 'em. We was just drivin' out there to apologize for any misunderstandings, and they stopped us cold in the road. We got out of the car to say our apologies, see, and they ganged up on us with clubs and chains and stuff, and we battled with 'em for—I don't know, maybe half an hour. Dom and Franco and Augie was rendered subconscious by their clubs, and smack in the middle of it them rednecks hauled out their artillery, and it was like World War II all over again, all the shootin' and blastin'. They shot up our vehicle—like to have ruint it and kilt us."

Alice clapped her hand over her mouth and her face turned white.

There was a pause while Big Ed shifted his cigar. "How many of 'em was there?"

Gino gestured wildly. "I dunno exactly, Boss. They was comin' so thick and fast who's countin'? At least twenty. Maybe thirty."

"Where did it happen?"

"Like, a mile or two from the meat company."

Big Ed said, "Now this next part is important, so don't make no mistakes." He cleared his throat and spoke softly. "Anybody else see it?"

Gino glowed. "That's the best part, Boss. Nobody else seen nothin'."

Big Ed released his held breath and smiled broadly. "That's good. Anybody on their side get hurt?"

"Naw, see, we was careful. It was them done all the shootin' and all the hittin'."

"Smart! Did you get the names of the guys who done it?"

"Like, who's takin' names when they're beatin' on you with baseball bats and shootin' the vehicle to pieces."

"Can you finger 'em if you see 'em again?"

"Yeah, oh, yeah, sure. That main one was the pencil-neck who done all their talkin' at the organization meetin' at the church. Name's Elbert. Yeah. Elbert."

Big Ed said, "Did he make any threats that other people heard in that church meetin'?"

"Yeah, oh sure, he threatened us if we ever came out there again. And that ain't the best part."

Big Ed plucked the cigar from his mouth and waited breathlessly. "Yeah, go on."

Gino spoke slowly, accenting each word. "He robbed about two grand from us."

Big Ed sat bolt upright. "Where'd you get two grand? You been dippin'?"

"Boss, you do me pain," Gino said, and he winced. "He robbed us of all our artillery."

"What! All of it?"

"Yeah. All fourteen heaters and the two choppers."

"They took *all* your artillery? Youse guys is without self-protection?"

"Yeah, right. Send us more. Dom and Franco don't sleep good without their artillery under their pillow."

"Yeah, yeah, okay." Big Ed knocked the cold ash from his cigar, and began thinking in big, big terms. "Now what I'm goin' to do," he said grandly, "is get Hugo. He'll get Tiny and about fifteen of our guys, and I'm goin' to send 'em on an airplane so they'll get there tomorrow. That's so's you got the same number of guys as they got."

Gino swallowed. "Uh, Boss, uh, I don't figger we'll need—"

Big Ed cut him off. "After that, what I'm gonna do, I'm gonna have Ferdie fill out an unfair labor practice charge, and charge 'em with everything from attempted murder to highway robbery. Then I'm goin' down to the labor board office and file it, and that'll force Hughie to send out a bunch of his investigators and mediators. It'll take a few days for 'em to get there, so while you're waitin', you get Hugo and his bunch to defend you guys. Do you get my meanin'?"

"You mean another unfair labor charge?"

Big Ed stuck the cigar back in his mouth. "Yeah. You gotta be careful that they start it, like last time. And no witnesses if you can avoid it, just like last time. You understand?"

"Yeah, Boss."

"Okay. I'm gonna put Irene on the phone now and you give her the phone number where I can get you. Okay?"

"Yeah, right, Boss."

Big Ed yelled, "Irene, you out there?"

A muffled voice called, "Yeah, gimme a minit already." A minute later she rotated through the door. "So what's the deal?" she said, and continued grinding her gum.

"Tell Ferdie to get in here, and then get on the phone at your desk and take this number from Gino."

She turned and screeched, "Ferdie, like, get in here."

Ferdie appeared quickly and stood by Big Ed's desk waiting.

Irene went back to the reception room and picked up the phone. "Awright, so what's the telephone number already," she asked, and laboriously began to write on a pad with a yellow pencil. "Not so fast! You goin' to a fire already? Start with the first number." She wrote further. "All right. I got it. Seven. What's next?"

Big Ed signalled and Ferdie closed the door.

Big Ed shifted his cigar again. "Gino just called. He done it! We got us an unfair labor charge. Thirty or forty of their guys beat up on Gino and our guys, shot up their car, and like to of killed them all. Stole all their artillery. Franco and Dom're in the hospital."

Ferdie's head jerked forward. "The hospital?"

"Yeah. Their guys used clubs and tire irons and chains. Now what you do, you get Hugo and about fif-

90

teen of our guys. Get 'em on an airplane today. Arrange for a hotel out there. Then write out an unfair labor charge against the meat company out there. Attempted murder, robbery, assault, battery—everything you can think of. Then you and I take it down to the labor board and get Hughie to send out an official United States Labor Department team of investigators and mediators."

Big Ed leaned back proudly in his big chair and paused while he envisioned government mediators rising majestically at the mediation table to look down their noses and condemn the Clearwater Meat Company for their cruelty to the innocent union negotiators.

"Anything else, Boss?" Ferdie asked.

"Yeah. Send some new artillery out to Gino and the boys. Fourteen heaters and two choppers."

Ferdie's forehead wrinkled. "They already got artillery."

"Not no more. The rednecks robbed 'em."

"*What!*"

"Broad daylight, right out on a country road." Big Ed looked righteous.

Ferdie raised one eyebrow. "Them rednecks out there took all that artillery away from Augie and Dom and Franco and the others, and put two of 'em in the hospital? Without our guys got in one lick, or shot nobody?"

"Vicious gang," Big Ed said solemnly. "Now git goin'."

"Right, Boss."

•ₒ ∘ ° •ₒ

In Lewiston, the instant Gino and Big Ed hung up the phones, Alice's fingers flew. She rammed three plugs into the switchboard and waited, wide-eyed and white-faced.

"Louise, you there? Clara? Phoebe?"

"Alice! Why, you sound like you've seen a ghost!"

"Worse," Alice hissed. "You are absolutely, positively not going to believe this. Why, I just heard it right here with my own two ears. Mobs and communists and Nazis and guns and beatings and hospitals—just positively, absolutely cannot believe it!"

Rich silence gripped the phone lines while Louise, Clara, and Phoebe breathed lightly so they could hear clearly, eyes aglow in anticipation.

Louise Quimby was wiry, hatchet-faced, thin-lipped, and direct. She married Norman Quimby, who was rotund and portly, had a fringe of hair, and was mild and quiet. He ran for mayor four times, lost each time, and decided running the town newspaper was what he needed for awhile before running for mayor again, so he could get his name out before the public a lot. He borrowed money from Louise's inheritance, bought the *Lewiston Gazette*, which published three times a week, and since it was her money, Louise was soon running the newspaper as well as Norman.

Clara Milligan was mousy and slightly round shouldered, and was never still, with her quick, nervous movements. She was married to Clyde Milligan, the county sheriff. Clyde had long since discovered that being reelected sheriff had more to do with being seen everywhere, and being on the radio and in the newspaper every time he could, than being a fearless law enforcer. He never missed a chance to make a speech or have his picture taken, and except for Clara's unending vigilance and constant haranguing he would have been blissfully unaware of half the crimes and criminals he was sworn to handle as sheriff. It was Clara and the Lewiston switchboard that tracked down Bernice McGwire's lost sow and twelve piglets, exposed the thieves that stole Swensen's Holstein heifer, caught the bootleggers that spiked the punch at the Moose Lodge summer carnival, and set up the roadblock that stopped and caught the crooks that robbed the gas station in Clarkston, across the river, and made a run for it. She made certain Clyde got the credit, and never let him forget who was really running the law in Lewiston.

Phoebe Nielsen was tall and square. She dressed in overalls and long-sleeved woolen shirts, tied her hair back with a shoelace, wore cowboy boots, grinned a lot, and whacked people on the back and slapped her thigh when she told jokes. She had a big, round, open face with slightly gapped teeth. Her nose turned up slightly, and when you thought of her face, somehow you thought of Porky Pig. She had been widowed thirteen years earlier when her lumberjack husband Niels went out on the Clearwater to clear out a logjam and was never seen again. Some said they saw him sneak on across to Clarkston and head for Spokane, but nobody could prove it. So Phoebe declared herself a widow, got the job as postmistress in Lewiston to support herself, and soon knew most of what was going on in the county by reading the return addresses on the envelopes when she sorted the mail. She also mastered the art of steaming open and re-sealing envelopes without leaving a trace, and five nights a week took the most interesting envelopes home with her before delivering them the next day.

The combination of the four of them—Alice at the switchboard, Louise running the newspaper, Clara running the sheriff, and Phoebe handling the mail—made strong men in high places tremble at mention of their names.

"What happened?" Louise exclaimed.

"You remember when Buster came back off the mail route and told me about the Nazis and communists going out to Hollis to join the union?"

"Yeah," Phoebe said. "He told me too."

"Well, yesterday it happened!"

"What happened?" Clara inquired.

"The Nazi communists went out there and they got attacked! That's what happened. Hundreds of men! They got beat with clubs and chains, and then their car got shot with bullets, and two of them are in the hospital."

Alice paused with her chin thrust out and her mouth puckered while she waited for that to hit bottom.

"By who?" inquired Louise.

"Elbert and about fifty others."

"Elbert!" exclaimed Clara. "Well, if Elbert done it, they likely had it coming."

Alice continued. "So the Chicago Nazi communists are sending out another hundred men with artillery."

Alice heard three gasps, and continued.

"They're coming in on airplanes, right here at Lewiston."

Alice paused to glance at her switchboard. Lights were flashing everywhere as the morning calls piled up.

"I've only got a minute," she said hurriedly. "The airplanes are coming in sometime tomorrow with all those Nazi communists. You know what *that* means."

"Yes. Sure. Of course." Louise, Clara, and Phoebe each stared blankly into space, unwilling to admit they did not know what *that* meant.

"And of course you all know your patriotic duty."

"Certainly. Absolutely. Without question." They stared into space again.

"I know you'll do right," Alice concluded. Then she said, "Phoebe, the very instant you see Buster, you tell him it is a life and death emergency that he call me. I'll wait all night for the call if I have to. You tell him."

"I will," Phoebe promised, and Alice jerked all three plugs out of the switchboard and quickly began working on the flashing red lights.

Louise fairly flew the three blocks to the *Gazette* office. "Harvey," she said to the chief typesetter, "get onto that machine. We've got headlines and the lead story for the next edition."

Harvey sighed and settled down to the big, clickity-clack machine, and his fingers flew while she spoke.

Norman walked in just as she finished.

"Got something?"

"Your headlines for the next edition, day after tomorrow. Biggest scoop ever."

"Yeah? What's up?"

"Nazi communist gangsters, robbery, attempted murder, shootings, beatings, people hospitalized. That's what's up. Where have you been?"

"Down at the dog pound. Hester lost her dog again. Five-dollar reward for Cuddles. Where'd you get all this Nazi stuff?"

"I've got my sources. You better get on out to Hollis tomorrow. There's going to be fireworks out there between the Nazi communists and Abe. Get right in the middle of it, with a pencil and notebook, and you'll get the biggest story since Lewis and Clark!"

When Alice pulled the plugs on the conference call, Clara immediately put in a call to Clyde at the sheriff's office.

"There was a terrible battle out at Hollis this morning! There's some men in the hospital right now. Tomorrow, hundreds of Nazi communists are coming in planes out at the airport. Now, Clyde, you set up a secret trap out there. Deputize Chigger and a bunch of other lumber-jacks and don't let on until you got all them Nazis and communists in one place, and then you pounce and arrest 'em."

"We don't have enough jail space."

"We'll use the basement in the Methodist church and the new high school gym."

"Yes ma'am," Clyde said meekly. He hung up the phone and headed for the newspaper office to get a pho-tographer to go with him to the hospital while he got the facts from whoever was there. He stopped only long enough to comb his hair and put his official sheriff's hat on, cocked slightly over his right eye so he looked both brave and a little dangerous. He had learned that impressed people when they saw his picture in the *Gazette*.

When Clyde hung up, Clara muttered to herself, "That oughta do it," and stared out the window for a minute. "I wonder what's goin' to happen tomorrow when everybody hits Hollis." She shook her head for a moment. "Oughta be interestin'."

CHAPTER 7

"Yeah, I'm Tom Bradley. Why?"

Bradley eyed Hugo suspiciously. His words echoed in the cavernous airplane hangar at Gowen Field, Boise, Idaho, where Bradley parked his ten single-engine Bradley Charter Air Service airplanes and did his repairs and maintenance. The weathered sign on the front of the hangar said WE DELIVER ANYTHING ANYTIME ANYWHERE, and in one corner one of his pilots had scrawled "Let's see the big boys try it." None of the regular airlines had air service from Boise to Lewiston. Air travellers to Lewiston had to use Bradley's charter service.

Bradley reached for a filthy, old, torn piece of towel hanging from the hip pocket of his dirty coveralls and began wiping at the grease and oil that covered his hands and wrists. His three-day growth of beard stubble wiggled when he talked.

Hugo looked irritated. "You run this here Bradley company?"

Bradley puckered his mouth for a moment while he considered. "Maybe I do and maybe I don't. Who're you?" Three or four of his mechanics and pilots stopped working on airplanes and sauntered over.

"I'm Hugo. Did Ferdie call about me?"

Bradley's mouth dropped open. *"You're Hugo?"* He stared at Hugo's brown suit—the black pinstripes, black shoes with white trim, and the fedora hat. He stood six feet five inches, 325 pounds.

Hugo looked irritated. "You got grease in yer ears? Yeah, I'm Hugo. Did Ferdie call?" Hugo glanced at the airplanes and grimaced.

Eight of Bradley's planes could carry five passengers each. The last two were ancient double wingers with a lot of patches, and had the front seats removed to make cargo space that ran clear back to the rear seat where the pilot sat. The old biplanes were used to haul DDT to the forest ranger stations all over the state to kill termites, and occasionally they were used to haul medicine, or small animals, or injured people, or whatever needed fast hauling to places other airlines would not or could not go.

The worst delivery Bradley could remember was hauling a six-hundred-pound mama grizzly bear and her two cubs from Challis to the Idaho Falls Zoo. The Challis forest ranger tied the mama with rope. At four thousand feet above the Rock Mountains, mama chewed through the knots and showed up between Bradley's feet with a roar that drowned out the airplane engine. Bradley made the last 278 miles doing incomparable aerial acrobatics, and the Idaho Falls air terminal closed down for two hours and twenty minutes after he landed and leaped from the airplane with a mad mama grizzly and two terrified cubs three steps behind.

"Yeah, someone named Ferdie called," Bradley replied. "Said a whole bunch of guys was comin' in on the 6:55 this mornin' from Chicago. They here?"

"Yeah," Hugo grunted. "In the office."

Bradley followed him through the scarred door and stopped dead in his tracks, eyes bugging. "These are the guys we're supposed to fly up to Lewiston?" Bradley gaped.

Hugo frowned. "Somethin' wrong with 'em? Ferdie told you sixteen guys, we got sixteen guys. So what's the problem?"

Hugo was the smallest of them. Tiny was the largest, at seven feet and 420 pounds. The average height was six feet eight inches, the average weight, 365 pounds. Each had a bulging suitcase, and carried an instrument case— saxophone, trombone, or violin.

"Wow!" breathed Bradley. "We figured four planes, four guys each, with one plane for luggage. Ferdie didn't tell us we was gonna be haulin' about five tons of bodies and their luggage besides."

"Yeah, well, so what're you goin' to do about it? We got appointments."

Bradley shook his head. "We're goin' to have to use every plane, includin' the old cargo bi-wingers. It'll cost you more."

Hugo shrugged. "We'll pay what Ferdie said. Call him if it's more. Meantime, we fly outta here, like in the next ten minutes."

Bradley swallowed hard and studied Tiny. Tiny's jaw and chin thrust out further than his nose. His eyes peered from beneath heavy brows, and he could look through most standard keyholes with both eyes at once. His left ear was cauliflowered, and his right one partly missing—bitten off years ago when he was a carnival wrestler. His arms hung loosely at his sides, and he could scratch either knee without bending. He could bear hug a fifty-five gallon barrel of beer off the ground, and no one could count the number of men Tiny had squeezed into unconsciousness, once he got them inside those massive arms. His smile made strong men stare, women gasp, and children whimper. His suit was sky blue, with black and white pinstripes.

Bradley noticed all the musical instrument cases. "These guys play in a band or somethin'?" he asked.

Tiny patted his violin case.

Hugo smiled. "They play real good."

"Yeah, well, I'll have to call Roy and Chuck and Clarence," Bradley said. "We'll need three more pilots. And I'll have to call Ferdie to get more money."

"Yeah, you do that," Hugo said, "while we're loadin'. Where's the planes?"

"You saw 'em right out in the hangar. All ten of 'em."

Hugo's jaw hit his chest. "Ten planes? You call them *airplanes?*"

Bradley stood straight. "Yeah, them's planes. Good ones. You don't like 'em, the deal's off. Take it or leave it. It don't make us no never mind."

Hugo led his column back into the hangar while Bradley telephoned Ferdie.

At 11:10 A.M., three hundred twenty miles north of Boise, Bradley spoke into his radio transmitter. "Bradley calling Lewiston airport. Homer, you there?"

A minute later a voice crackled. "Tom, that you comin' in from the south?"

"Yeah."

"Holy mackerel, what've you got? The whole Army Air Corps?"

"There's ten of us. How's the field?"

The Lewiston airport was on a plateau east of town. They kept a bulldozer with a front end blade handy to keep the dirt as level as possible, fill in badger holes, and scrape off snow in the winter. After a rain, they had to wait for it to dry before they graded out the gullies and hollows again.

"Pretty good. Watch at the north end. Some goldanged gophers and two badgers got some holes down there. We set out some baits but we ain't got 'em all yet."

"You got someone named Gino there waiting for a bunch of guys from Chicago?"

"Yeah. In a school bus?"

Bradley's head jerked forward. "In a *what?*"

"School bus. Don't ask."

"Okay. We're loaded heavy, so we're coming straight in."

Whatever their shortcomings, Tom Bradley and his pilots could put a small plane down anywhere there was one hundred feet of open, flat surface. Each pilot had flown fighter planes in World War II in combat conditions. In swift succession they lined up with the field, settled, touched down gently, then hit the brakes or reversed their propellers, and stopped.

With expressions of eternal gratitude to whatever powers preside in the heavens above, Hugo crawled out of Bradley's plane and looked lovingly at the dirt under his feet. The others followed, except for Tiny. They had to help him unfold from the cramped freight bay in one of the old biwingers, with his eyes watering and nose running from the strong DDT fumes that lingered inside.

Gino walked out of the shack where Homer handled all the airport business, followed by Tony and the others, and they walked hastily to Hugo. "Did you bring us new artillery?"

Hugo nodded. "Yeah. Where we stayin'?"

"At the Lumberjack hotel, and six at the motel in town. Where's the artillery?"

"In them instrument cases. Why ain't we stayin' one place or the other?"

"Hotel's got some rooms taken and the motel partly burned down. Now, like, let's get loaded. We got to visit a meat company today, now that we got youse guys and our artillery."

"Right. Where's the cars?"

"No cars. We're ridin' in a school bus."

Hugo's face screwed into a prune. "That ain't funny."

"Like, who's bein' funny?" Gino exclaimed. "Lewiston ain't got no cars for rent, and Big Ed ain't paying for new ones. We had three choices. A cattle truck without no seats and with green stuff in it that stank, or an old city garbage truck, or a school bus with seats. So we're ridin' in a school bus. Get your stuff."

Bradley and his pilots watched the twenty-three men heft their luggage and instrument cases and disappear around the airfield shack. Bradley led his pilots inside, where Homer sat by the radio.

"What's goin' on here?" Bradley asked. "Them guys ain't no dance band."

Homer shook his head. "Don't rightly know it all yet, but it looks like we got us a war up here."

Bradley scratched his beard stubble. "Well, me and my guys seen enough of war flyin' fighters in Europe. I'll see you later."

103

Outside, Hugo rounded the corner of the shack and stopped cold.

A 1928 Dodge school bus faced the building. Rust had decimated the yellow paint and eaten large holes in both front fenders. The windshield was gone, along with both headlights. Half the windows were gone, the others broken, and the tires were smooth. Springs and padding gaped through holes in the upholstery of every one of the thirty-two seats. The huge, faint, lingering outline of the head of a badger could be seen on both sides, with lettering, LEWISTON HIGH SCHOOL BADGERS, still discernible if one cared to study it. The door sat crooked in the frame.

Hugo looked like he'd sucked a sour pickle. "We're goin' in this pile of junk?"

"You'd like the cattle truck maybe?"

Twenty minutes later Dom rode the brake pedal with all his weight until the bus slowly squealed and clattered to a stop in front of the Lumberjack. Gino led the way upstairs, and Hugo and nine others threw their suitcases and instrument cases into five rooms, then gathered in Gino's room.

"So where's the artillery?" Gino said. "Dom and Franco ain't been sleepin' good without it."

Two minutes later Gino and his six smiled broadly with the feel of .45 caliber Colt automatics in their shoulder holsters and another in their hip pockets. They closed two trombone cases and three saxophone cases containing Thompson submachine guns and grabbed the handles.

"Like comin' home," Gino beamed. "So let's get on down to the Aloha and then we go to the meat company." Ten minutes later they all clambered off the bus and Hugo stood wide-eyed at the sight of the construction crew finishing the burned wing of the Aloha.

"This is where these six guys are stayin'?" Hugo asked in disbelief.

"Yeah, right," Gino said defensively. "They had a fire and they're fixin' it, and they got that wing over there in good shape, see." He pointed. "They got good rooms, if it don't rain. And we ain't had no rain yet."

Fifteen minutes later they all gathered back at the bus. "Okay," Gino said, "now Big Ed says we're supposed to go see if we can arrange another meetin' with the employees of the meat company so's they can assault us again. Only this time," he paused to pat the bulge of his shoulder holster, "we ain't without self-protection."

Three minutes later Dom released the emergency brake and threw all his weight onto the steering wheel to turn the bus to the right, onto the dirt road leading east, towards Hollis.

Back at the post office Phoebe stopped reading postcards long enough to call to Buster: "Alice says call her. Life or death."

Buster leaped to the phone on the worn pinewood desk and jerked the earpiece off the hook and waited.

"Number pleeuzz."

"Alice, Phoebe said—"

"Buster! Oh Buster, thank you for calling. Thank you." Her voice was pitched too high and was wavering with unquenchable emotion. "The pie. Did you like the pie? The last one—mountain blueberry?"

"Pie? Oh, yeah, sure; pie, good pie. Phoebe said—"

"Picked them last Sunday myself, right up there above the picnic grounds."

"Life or death."

"What?" Alice's face knitted in question.

"Life or death. Phoebe said life or death."

Flustered, Alice clasped her hand to her throat and her eyes opened wide. "Oh, I nearly forgot!" she exclaimed. "Those Nazi communists are coming in to the airport this morning and then they're going on out to Hollis and there's going to be a big battle about this union thing."

Buster gasped. "I got to get up there! I'll let you know soon as I get back."

Alice's voice rang. "Now Buster, you be careful. Don't you get hurt trying to be a hero. You hear me?"

"I'll be careful unless they start something," Buster breathed, and he slammed the earpiece back on the hook and sprinted for the door as fast as his stocky legs would go.

Across town, Clyde Milligan eased his Ford sedan against the curb in front of the big window with LEWIS-TON GAZETTE printed in large letters that were beginning to crumble and flake. On the side of the green Ford the words COUNTY SHERIFF were printed in large letters, with "Law and Order" in smaller letters beneath. Clyde walked into the *Gazette* office and waited a moment with his nose wrinkled at the smell of printer's ink and the racket of a printing press running in the back room.

"Norman, you and Walt comin'?" he finally called.

"Yeah, just a minute while I grab a pencil and note-book," Norman answered from behind a curtain that separated the front office from the printing presses. A moment later he pushed through the curtain, followed by Walt, who carried a canvas bag slung around his neck on a strap, inside of which was his big black box camera and a box of slides.

Walter Phipps was the handyman for the *Gazette*, which included being their official photographer. He was slightly hunch shouldered, wore thick glasses to correct an extreme case of nearsightedness, and was constantly squinting and pushing his glasses back up his nose.

"Let's go."

Two minutes later Clyde started the engine of the Ford, checked the rearview mirror to be certain no car was approaching, studied the street ahead to be certain it was also vacant, gave a hand signal that he was leaving the curb, and slowly eased out into the vacant street. He turned to Norman.

"Can't be too careful," he said. "Anybody sees the sheriff drivin' reckless, why, next thing you know, the whole county's speedin' and racin' around."

Norman nodded.

They continued east on Main Street, then south on Elm Street to connect with the road travelling to Hollis. Clyde pulled to a stop at the Fourth Street stop sign, looked both ways, checked his rearview mirror, examined the road straight ahead, and slowly eased across Fourth Street.

He scrooched his head around to look at Walt in the backseat. "Can't be too careful," he said. "Got to check all four ways at a stop sign. Anybody sees the sheriff not checkin', why, next thing you know, you just as well take all the stop signs down and let folks drive wild."

Walt nodded and toyed with his camera.

Suddenly Norman yelled, "Watch out, Clyde," and Clyde jerked around in time to hit the brakes and slide the Ford to a stop in the street.

"I believe you missed it," Norman said, and released pent-up breath.

"What was it?"

"Somethin' small and white, runnin'." Norman hung his head out the window on his side and watched. A small, white poodle dog with manicured paws and a groomed coat and a pink ribbon between its ears proudly arched its head and trotted towards the curb.

"Why, that's Hester's pup," Clyde exclaimed. "There's a five-dollar reward on Cuddles." He quickly parked the Ford against the curb. "Come on. We got to get it. Walt, grab that camera and come a-runnin'."

"We don't have time," Norman protested. "We're supposed to get out to Hollis and cover the news story."

"You just don't understand," Clyde insisted. "We got Walt and his camera right here, and you run the newspaper. If we catch Cuddles and return her to Hester, why, we'll have our picture right on the front page, handin' that poor darlin' puppy back to Hester, and she'll be cryin' and we'll look humble, and that'll fetch at least five hundred votes at the next election."

"If we miss the fireworks out at Hollis, it won't make no difference about Cuddles," Norman insisted. "Louise'll kill us both. Then we *will* be on the front page. Besides, it's that five-dollar reward you're after, and a regular police officer can't get reward money for doin' his duty." Clyde shook his head violently. "It ain't the reward money. You can have that." He paused to weigh it out in his mind.

Hester Trimble was the president of the Daughters of the Pioneers, and had been for forty-eight years. With 571 members, and each with a telephone, the Daughters had elected and un-elected more politicians than any other organization in the county.

"No," Clyde declared, "we got to do our duty to Lewiston before we start for Hollis. Now you two get out, and Walt, bring the camera."

Norman sighed and got out, and Walt followed with his bag, and all three men stopped at the clatter and rattle of an ancient bus travelling east on the Hollis road, one block ahead.

"Isn't that the old high school bus?" Walt said, with eyes squinted as they watched the bus weave through the intersection and disappear.

"Yeah, it is," Norman confirmed.

"What's it doin' on the Hollis road?" Clyde pondered. "I figured it was junk."

"I don't know," Norman answered.

Clyde turned and pointed. "There's Cuddles again, over there at the corner of Effie Barnstetter's house. Easy now, gentle, while we catch her."

Walt paused to watch the wrinkled old Chevy pickup, with US MAIL painted on the side with a stick, rattle up the road eastward towards Hollis, three minutes behind the school bus.

"There goes Buster on his mail run," he said to himself, and shoved a negative plate into his old box camera. He sighed and walked rapidly to catch up with Clyde and Norman, while Cuddles disappeared behind Effie's house.

Twenty-eight miles east, at the meat plant, Abe hung his yellow rubber apron on its peg in the boiler room and tugged at his big rubber boots. "Headin' home?" he asked Elbert.

"Yeah, soon. I gotta stop at Jake Sorba's first."

Abe looked up. "He got trouble?"

"Naw, he's got a howl in the U-joint on his pickup. Just needs a wrench I got that'll handle them master bolts."

"Tell him his eight geese'll be finished in the smoke-house by Monday."

"Yep. Jack and Bill comin' in tomorrow?"

"Yeah. Monday okay for you?"

"I'll be here rarin' to go."

Elbert hugged Beth as he passed through the office, and Beth shook her head.

"What was that for?" she asked.

"Make Abe jealous," Elbert said, and grinned.

"Get outta here," she said gruffly, and grinned back at him as he walked out the door and climbed into his pickup truck.

By the time he got to Feeney's he was in the third chorus of "Tennessee Waltz," and he waved at Emma as his pickup jostled past.

"My friend stolt my true love from me.

"I rememberrrrrr . . ." he held the high note until his voice cracked, then continued, "the night, and the Tennessee Waltz,

"Now I know just how much I have lost,

"Yes, I lost my little darlin' . . ."

He finished all four verses and one he had made up himself, and was just starting over again when suddenly he stopped singing and took his foot off the gas pedal.

"What is *that?*" he muttered under his breath.

Coming towards him, weaving all over the road, was the old Lewiston Badger school bus, both headlights and windshield missing.

Elbert stopped and leaned over the steering wheel of his pickup, staring.

Inside the bus Dom caught sight of the pickup between the zig and the zag as he battled to hold the bus on the road, and a flicker of remembrance jolted him.

"Hey," he hollered to Gino, who was seated two rows back. "Ain't that the truck that we had the trouble with before?"

Gino lunged out of his seat, down by Dom, and thrust his head clear out the hole where the windshield should have been.

"Slow down," he called back to Dom. "I can't tell the way this thing keeps jumpin' all over the road."

Dom slowed.

Gino recoiled clear back two rows, trembling, face white. "That's him! That's the one."

Franco rounded his mouth and blew air.

Hugo said, "That's who?"

"That's the guy that beat up on us last time."

"That was a mob, twenty or thirty guys."

"He's a mob," Gino blurted.

Hugo looked disgusted. "Dom, pull up right in front of his pickup. Tiny, get on up here."

The bus slowed and settled and squealed to a stop thirty feet from Elbert's pickup while Elbert peered through the missing windshield and his eyes popped and his mouth dropped open as he recognized Dom, then Gino.

"Them guys again?" he said to himself. "Guess I better talk to 'em." He opened the pickup door and got out.

Inside the bus, Tiny made his way forward, and stood inside the door while Hugo said, "This here's the guy what led the mob that beat up on Dom and Franco and the others. Go get him. Hug him down."

Tiny thought for a minute and finally nodded. He grinned and flexed his massive hands in anticipation.

Elbert strode right up to the misfit door on the bus and banged on it. "Open up," he called. "Looks like we better talk some more, on account of we already told you we don't want no union out here."

Half a mile west, Buster crested a gentle rise in the road, talking to himself. "Hope I ain't too late gettin' to Abe and Beth. If them Nazi communists get there first . . ." He shook his head, and his mouth became a straight line as he stomped on the gas pedal to get full speed on the slight downhill grade. Then he saw the rear end of the old school bus in the middle of the road and eased up on the gas. "What in tarnation is *that?*" he exclaimed out loud.

While he watched, Elbert appeared at the bus door and Buster saw him slap it with the flat of his hand.

Inside the bus, Hugo grabbed the door lever and wrenched the door open. "Okay, get him, Tiny!" he exclaimed, and Tiny looked down at Elbert.

Elbert looked up at Tiny.

Tiny grinned, ducked his head, and stepped to the ground. He flexed his hands and took a step towards Elbert. Behind him Hugo and Dom and the whole load on the bus were hanging out the windows, shouting, "Get him, Tiny. Hug him down."

"Hold on," Elbert hollered. "I don't want no trouble. You fellas just turn this contraption around and head on back where you come from."

Tiny raised his arms.

Elbert's eyes narrowed. "Now lookee here, mister," he said, "I don't want no trouble, but the way you're doin' is startin' to irritate me. I don't want to get peeved, so just get back into that thing and get on outta here."

Tiny lunged, and Elbert stepped inside the massive arms and leaned forward, and jammed his forehead against Tiny's chest, and in two seconds he whipped four sledgehammer punches straight into Tiny's midsection, left, right, left, right, whump-whump-whump-whump!

Tiny grunted with each whump. On the second grunt he began to sag forward. On the third grunt he grabbed his stomach with both hands. On the fourth grunt he bent forward, nearly double, eyes bugged out, unable to breathe, frozen like a statue, nearly paralyzed, and his head dropped to the level of Elbert's shoulders.

Elbert dropped his right foot back about four inches, set himself, and swung a right hook with every pound he had. It caught Tiny just above his left ear. Tiny sighed and went limp and toppled over sideways. The ground trembled slightly as he hit, and he rolled partially on his back, with a look of total peace on his face.

Elbert looked at the suddenly white faces hanging out the bus windows. "Now see what you done? You got me peeved. Four of you git out here and git this guy loaded and . . ."

Hugo shouted, "*All of you, rush him, gang him!*" then lunged to the door and leaped out. Elbert got to the door half a second before Hugo's feet hit the ground and Elbert hit him twice, left, right, whump-whump, and Hugo dropped right beside Tiny and didn't move.

Two more men jammed their way through the door and Elbert caught the first one with a right, the second one with a left, and they went down and lay still. Two more shoved their way out and Elbert set his feet and twice more he swung from his heels and twice more men went down limp as rag dolls, rolling, and one of their pistols fell out of its holster and lay shiny in the dust.

The next two men started out the door and Elbert reset his feet and looked up. The men swallowed hard and looked down at him, and saw the thunder and lightning in his eyes. They looked at Tiny and Hugo, and the other four men laid out, and one looked at the other and they slowly backed up into the bus.

Behind the bus, Buster had witnessed the entire battle. "Well," he said matter-of-factly, "they went and done it. They peeved Elbert."

Elbert stood outside the bus door waiting for the next rush, when Franco stepped into the door frame, reached inside his coat, and pulled out his pistol.

Instantly Elbert scooped up the pistol that had fallen from the sixth man, and swung it up to point directly at the fourth button on Franco's black dress shirt.

"Now goldang it," Elbert bellowed, "you throw down that pistol right now. You're gettin' me real mad. Throw it down!"

Franco gulped. "Yessir," he breathed, and threw the pistol out the door and backed up inside the bus. Elbert leaped inside the door and Franco stumbled backwards and everybody inside the bus scrambled to the rear, all scrunched into a single bunch.

"Any of the rest of you got guns, throw 'em out the windows right now!" He waved the pistol at them.

Behind them, Buster's head jerked forward in disbelief as forty-three pistols came flying out the windows on both sides of the bus, followed by sixteen musical instrument cases.

"Okay," Elbert bawled, "now you first six guys git out there and load up them guys outside. Go on. Git."

Three minutes later the six unconscious men were sprawled in the first six seats, while the other seventeen were jammed in the bus behind them, pasty-faced and wide-eyed.

Outside, half a mile behind Buster, Clyde crested the gentle rise and lifted his foot from the gas pedal in the County Ford.

"What do you figger that is up ahead?" he asked Norman.

Norman peered, and Walt shoved his glasses back up his nose and leaned forward, eyes squinted. "Looks like Buster," Norman said, "but what in the world is that thing ahead of him?"

"Ain't that the old Badger high school bus? Remember, from when we were on the high school team?" Walt said.

Clyde leaned over the steering wheel and narrowed his eyes for better focus. "By cracky, I think it is!" Suddenly he jerked backwards. "Didn't I hear them guys from back east bought that old bus?" He stomped his foot back onto the gas pedal.

Inside the bus, Elbert threw his pistol out the nearest window and faced the crowd cowering in the rear. "I told you nice to go on back wherever you come from, but no, you just wouldn't listen, and you got ornery. I reckon there's only one way to cool you guys off so's you'll get out of Hollis and leave us alone." He settled into the driver's seat, cranked up the old engine, ground the gears into low, and the tired old bus groaned as it moved forward.

From the road, the Clearwater River was just over sixty yards south, where it rolled wide and gentle for about forty feet, then narrowed. Two great boulders thrust above the surface, and many more beneath the surface, roiled the river into white water. Thirty feet further the river suddenly widened again, then ran smooth and slow and shallow for nearly half a mile. From the road the ground sloped gently to the river with a covering of sagebrush, a few rocks, some new-growth white pines about waist high, and some scrub oak.

Elbert wrenched the steering wheel to the right and the bus lumbered off the road and started down the slope to the river, gaining speed as it lurched through the brush and over the rocks. Fifteen yards later Elbert heard muttering from the bunch behind him, and finally one of them shouted above the noise of the bouncing and clattering, "What're you, crazy or somethin'?"

Elbert broke into verse one of "Tennessee Waltz," grinning from ear to ear, whipping the wheel back and forth to avoid occasional boulders.

Behind the bus, up on the road, Clyde slid the sheriff's car to a standstill and leaped out. "Why, that bus is headed smack dab for the river!"

From his mail truck Buster stared for a moment, then suddenly burst into rib-splitting laughter.

From the rear of the bus a dozen panic-stricken voices joined chorus. "STOP THIS THING. YOU'RE NUTS!"

"When an old friend I happened to see,

"I introduced him to my darlin',

"And while they was dancin' . . ."

Elbert was singing at the top of his lungs.

Walt leaped from the sheriff's car, his big camera bag banging on his side, and ran pell-mell through the brush, down the incline towards the river, Norman right behind. Clyde fell in behind them.

Inside the bus was a storm of shouts. "STOP! WE'LL LEAVE TOWN! STOP!"

Elbert ignored it. ". . . my friend stolt my true love from me . . .

"I rememberrrrrr . . ." Elbert held the high note until his voice cracked while he flipped the gearshift into neutral and turned off the key. The bus hit twenty miles an hour, ten yards from the river. At five yards, Elbert opened the door.

"The night and the Tennessee Waltz . . ."

He dived out the open door and rolled onto his feet as the battered old bus plowed into the Clearwater. It threw spray fifty feet into the air and a curtain of water splattered in through the missing windshield. The bus slowed a little, turned slightly to the right with the current, but continued on, while cold river water swirled through the open door. Fifteen feet from shore, the river reached the window level, and at twenty feet only the top two feet of the bus showed above the surface. It settled to a full stop, held for a moment, then began drifting slowly with the current.

Inside, panic turned to pandemonium. Seventeen men scrambled for windows and battled their way through, then climbed onto the top of the bus like a bunch of drowned rats. When the cold water reached Tiny and Hugo and the last four, they shook the cobwebs out of their brains and sat up in their seats to peer at a world gone crazy. They turned in time to see the last of the others kick their way through the windows, and they followed them.

Elbert counted until all twenty-three were on top of the bus as it slowly worked west with the current. The shouts turned to frantic screams. "HELP! GIT THE NAVY! GIT THE FIRE DEPARTMENT! WE CAN'T SWIM."

Walt stormed up beside Elbert, panting, and wordlessly jerked out his camera and began clicking and changing plates at record speed. Norman stopped right behind Walt, holding his sides from running, and gasped, "What happened? I'm from the newspaper." He had his pencil and notebook ready.

Elbert looked at him with a curled lip. "Norman, I know dang well you're from the newspaper."

Clyde labored up behind, yelling, "Stop all this, in the name of the law."

Elbert grinned at him. "It's stopped, or will be when it hits them two big rocks."

The bus settled against the two great boulders, caught precariously, and stopped.

"How are we going to get those men ashore?" Clyde exclaimed, trying to control his breathing.

"Easy," Elbert answered. He turned to the men on the bus and shouted: "Just jump in the river and go with the current. Thirty feet on down she's wide and shallow and you can walk out. Town's only twenty-six miles thataway, and if you git started now you can make it by midnight."

"WE CAN'T SWIM!"

Elbert yelled back, "Just jump and hold yer breath. It ain't even up to your knees, thirty feet on down."

The bus shifted, the current caught it, and it rolled. Horrendous shouts filled the air as all twenty-three men hit the water. A moment later it appeared as though the Clearwater River had magically changed to something alive, with arms and legs thrashing and flailing the water to a froth, with heads bobbing up and down in the midst of it all.

Buster came charging from the road, laughing so hard he had to sit down.

Clyde yelled at Walt, "Wait a dang minute with that camera," and he ran down to the water and waded in up to his knees and gave his best profile to Walt with the bus and the floundering men in the background. He didn't know whether to look like he was rescuing the swimmers or was the one that put them in the river, but he did know that the picture would be seen by everybody within five hundred miles, and that was what was important. Walt clicked, then trotted on down to see if the men got out of the river.

As the river widened and slowed, one by one they got their feet on the bottom and made their way to the bank, dripping, sloshing, water streaming from their pin-striped suits. They collapsed and lay prostrate on the bank, heedless of the mud.

Elbert trotted up to them. "Best get started," he said pleasantly. "Bears roam these parts at night."

Groans filled the air. A few heads raised and squinted eyes looked hatefully at Elbert.

"'Course I don't reckon there's any real danger," Elbert continued. "There wasn't more'n seven folks got et by bears by this time last year. See, in May and June they come out of their long winter sleep hungrier'n sin, and ready to eat anything that moves. Makes me kinda fearful what would happen if about four of them big grizzlies happened onto a whole mob of walkin' dinners."

Hugo stirred and rose to his knees.

"'Course," Elbert continued matter-of-factly, "there's ways to protect yourself. Bears hate singin', and worst of all, they hate religious singin'."

He paused, and his face puckered in deep thought for just a moment. "Tell you what," he announced, "you gents all gather round here, and I'll teach you a song that'll keep the bears away, guaranteed."

Twenty-three voices raised in protest.

Elbert walked over to Hugo, grabbed him under his arms, and hoisted him to his feet. He straightened Hugo's tie and brushed at the mud and pine needles stuck to his suit. Then he set his feet and balled his right hand into a fist and raised it slightly. "You'd like to learn a song to keep the bears away, wouldn't you?"

Hugo looked down at the clenched fist and slowly nodded his head.

"I knew it," Elbert grinned. "Now all you other gents git on over here before I git peeved again."

Twenty seconds later Elbert looked at the semicircle of muddy, dirty, soaked, murderous men, and grinned.

"Good. Now I'm goin' to lead you in the first verse of that guaranteed bear scarin' song, 'We Shall Gather at the River.'"

CHAPTER 8

There is enchantment at 2:55 A.M. in the deep hush of a clear, still night on the Clearwater. Beneath a full moon waxing, nighthawks perform a flawless ballet as they pirouette and dart and glide on soft, silent wings. The river divides the world, a winding, graceful, sparkling ribbon cradled by the rise of the mountains on either side. Those who know say that the first stirring of the morning breeze is God passing nearby, and if you sit quietly, and listen with your soul, you can hear him whisper in the pines, "It is mine, and it is good."

The nighthawks, and the full moon waxing, and the voice of God in the pines were a total loss to the twenty-three men who cursed and limped and staggered their way into the dark and quiet town of Lewiston as the big clock on the Lumberman's Bank tolled three times in the stillness. They followed the taillights of Clyde's Ford to the Aloha, where six of them dropped out of the ragged column and disappeared into dark rooms, while the others followed the taillights on to the Lumberjack. None of them spoke more than a word or two. Their voices had become raw twelve miles back, then stopped altogether on the eighty-seventh chorus of "We Shall Gather at the River."

Clyde slowed, but did not stop, at either the motel or the hotel. At his office he turned off the ignition and listened while the engine continued to fire for ten more seconds. He was unable to budge the gearshift out of low gear. The heat gauge had hit the red zone nineteen miles back, after travelling seven miles at two miles per hour, and Clyde was convinced the transmission had welded itself into low gear forever.

However, at that moment he did not care. He only knew that after seven hours of "We Shall Gather at the River" and nine hours of endless whimpering and whining from men with blistered feet and cramps in their leg muscles, he could think only of the overpowering luxury of cool, white cotton sheets, and a pillow.

Walt was stuffed in the front seat between Clyde and Norman, with the gearshift between his knees. The backseat and the trunk were jammed full to the roof with forty-four Colt pistols and sixteen instrument cases.

Norman popped open the passenger door and got out stiff, followed by Walt, who stood on legs that had long since lost circulation. He leaned against the car while one million needles tingled in his leg muscles.

Norman mumbled to Clyde. "See you tomorrow."

Clyde shook his head. "It's already tomorrow."

Norman set his course up the block to the *Lewiston Gazette*. Walt silently fell in behind, and they plodded slowly onward, the canvas bag bumping Walt's hip.

By one o'clock in the afternoon Walt had twenty-six photographs developed. By two-thirty Louise and Homer had set print for a special edition of the *Gazette*, the first special edition since the Japanese surrendered in World War II. The presses in the back room of the *Gazette* were ready to roll as soon as Walt's photos were cast on the lead cylinders. The four-inch headlines read: WAR ERUPTS ON THE CLEARWATER. In three-inch letters below came DEATH DEFYING ACCOUNT, in two-inch letters below that, BY LOUISE QUIMBY, ASSISTANT EDITOR, and in one-inch letters below that, TAKEN FROM THE FIRSTHAND ACCOUNTS OF EDITOR NORMAN QUIMBY AND SHERIFF CLYDE MILLIGAN. And below that, in small print, Photos by Walt.

The first six pages were Walt's photographs. Centered on page one was a photo of the Badger bus washed up against the big boulders in the river, with Gino and Hugo and Tiny and all the others soaked, bedraggled, frantically waving. The subtitle read, UNION ON THE ROCKS. The photographs were arranged in order, showing the step-by-step developments, the last of which was Elbert teaching the half-drowned men the chorus of "We Shall Gather at the River."

Following were four editorial pages, created by Louise after reading Norman's sketchy notes and having a talk with Clyde and Walt and Buster.

At 3:30 P.M. Louise picked up the phone at the *Gazette*.

"Alice, get Phoebe and Clara."

There was a pause while Alice pushed plugs, and then they all answered.

Louise indulged in one of her most dramatic pauses, then said in a quiet voice, "This is serious." Another pause that dripped drama. "It's the hand of Providence— that's the only reason Clyde and Norman are alive. Clyde brought back hundreds of pistols and at least fifty of those big new automatic guns the G-men use to get gangsters like John Dillinger."

For ten minutes her voice rose and fell in phrases that oozed drama all over the phone. As she slowed to a conclusion, her face must have resembled that of Joan of Arc when she made her defense at Rouen. "The Constitution of America has been saved. You all know what this means."

"Yes. Of course. Certainly."

"And you all know what to do?"

"No question. Immediately. Obviously."

Louise hung up. The other three sat for a moment, reaching to find the outer limits of the unbelievable plum that had dropped in their laps. The most colossal story since statehood, and they could be the first to stun the world with it. Each snatched up her phone.

By four o'clock crowds were gathering at the Lumberjack and the Aloha, craning necks to get a glimpse of the twenty-three infamous union Nazi communists inside. At eight o'clock Lou Gibney signed off the Lewiston radio station, and closed it down for the night. At ten past eight Lou was sitting in Marty's diner, waiting for a bowl of chili and a slab of apple pie.

Lou Gibney owned and operated the only radio station within eighty miles, KLI. He was also the sole employee. He was small and curly-headed with great soulful eyes and a resonant baritone voice that sounded like John Barrymore on the radio. He wrote his own scripts, sold airtime, kept the books, swept the place out twice a month, opened at six o'clock every morning, and closed it fourteen hours later.

Norman burst through the door. "Lou, I been looking all over for you."

Lou chewed his toothpick.

"We've got the biggest news story of the century. Big, Lou. Real big."

"What's up?"

"You heard about the union going up to get Abe to join?"

"I heard."

"Well, they sent a busload of men up there, and they got Elbert peeved, and he ran the whole load in the river."

Marty set a bowl of steaming chili in front of Lou, and Lou reached for the ketchup and a spoon.

"Yeah, go on."

"Well, we got pictures and a firsthand story. You've never seen the likes."

Lou closed one eye, blew on the first spoon load of chili, and carefully touched it with his tongue and instantly drew back. "Man, that's hot."

"Lou, you ain't listenin'. This story goes clear back to Chicago. Big union bosses. Guns. Nazis. Communists. The whole kit and kaboodle of 'em in the river today, in a bus. Elbert whupped about half of 'em. Big, Lou."

Lou turned the Heinz ketchup bottle upside down, whacked it on the bottom, and a blob of ketchup smacked into the chili. Lou wiped spots of chili off the counter with a paper napkin.

"Usual deal?"

"Uh, I figure this one's going to be at least triple circulation. So, uh, well, I figure half a cent for each copy above the average. Okay?"

Lou shook his head. "Nope. Usual deal. I plug it on my radio, I get one penny for every copy sold over average circulation."

Norman pondered, then shook his head. "Too much. Three quarters of a cent."

"Alice and the girls know about this?"

"They're right in the middle of it."

Lou puckered for a moment in thought. If Alice and the girls were on the phone with this story, circulation ought to skyrocket. "Okay, three quarters of a cent. Get me a copy of your newspaper by six in the morning and I'll see what I can do."

Norman nodded, shook hands to seal the deal, and hastily walked out. Lou walked to the pay phone on the wall, dropped his nickel and waited.

"Alice, what's the skinny on this union thing?" Then he settled back to listen for fifty-five minutes.

In the gray five o'clock dawn the newspaper delivery boys filled their bags with newspapers and delivered their routes to the awakening town, while Norman made the drops at the drugstore and the grocery store and then waited at the radio station at the edge of town until Lou rode in on his bicycle.

"Here she is," Norman said, and handed the special edition to Lou.

Lou looked at the pictures on the front page, thumbed through the rest of the photos, then scanned the four-page editorial.

He yawned and scratched his head. "Thanks. See you later."

At 5:50 A.M. Lou found an old warped record of the sound track for a John Wayne war movie of the attack on

127

Wake Island and dropped it on the turntable. He threw the switch and waited while his transmitter warmed up, then glanced out at the tower. At six o'clock he flicked the button on his microphone and settled onto the wooden chair with the back long since broken and gone and a worn-out cushion on the seat.

"Good morning everyone out there in happy land. This is Lou Gibney, broadscattering the best of everything there is to know. This morning we're not going to play 'The Star-Spangled Banner' like always to start the day right, because we've got a news bulletin that is so hot it puts the eyes of this entire nation on our own little community. We got us a war."

He turned up the volume on the record for six or eight seconds, and the sounds of planes diving and machine guns blasting reached eighty miles in every direction. Half the population within the reach of the radio station slowed for a moment with one eyebrow cocked in wonderment.

Lou turned down the volume and exchanged phonograph records. "Seems Chicago union organizers took a crack at Abe Jones's meat company up on the Clearwater at Hollis. Sent about a battalion of tough guys to do the job. They wound up in the Clearwater River, but were persuaded to leave their pistols—forty-four of them and sixteen tommy guns—up on the road."

He turned up the volume, and the sounds of raucous laughter went out over the airwaves for five seconds.

Logging trucks on narrow mountain roads pulled over and stopped while the drivers turned up the volume on their radios. Wives stopped turning pancakes on hot griddles. Fishermen slowed while they pulled nets. Farmers paused in driving milk cows into their milking stations.

"Okay," Lou continued, "got your attention? Give me ten minutes, I'll give you the details. After that, get the special edition of the *Lewiston Gazette*. Six pages of Walt's photographs and four pages of Louise's usual nonsense—the whole shebang."

At eight-fifteen Lou's phone rang.

"This is radio station KBOI in Boise. What's this we picked up about a war up there?"

At nine-fifty-five Norman's phone jangled. "This is the *Boise Herald*. Our switchboard's going crazy. What's going on up there?"

At noon Alice threw up her hands in despair. Her switchboard was humming, and lights were flashing with calls from Washington, Oregon, Montana, Wyoming, Nevada, Utah, Wisconsin, Texas, and California. By 3:30 P.M. she had slowly laid her head forward on her arms and by force of will ignored the impossible load jamming her switchboard.

•₀ ∘° •₀

The following day dawned dark and dreary in Chicago, with a drizzle of cold rain coming off Lake Michigan. People hurried from buses to offices with umbrellas and upturned collars.

Irene walked into the union office, dumped the mail and the morning *Chicago Tribune* onto her cluttered desktop, and shook her umbrella. Water showered Ferdie, her typewriter, and the mound of papers.

"Hey," Ferdie exclaimed, "shake that thing out in the hall."

"So yer gonna die from a little water?" she retorted.

"Look what you done to the mail and them papers."

Irene shrugged. "Yeah, yeah. They'll dry out. Who's to notice?"

She minced over to drop her still expanded umbrella in the corner, hang her raincoat on the coat tree, and flounce her hair.

Ferdie picked up the morning copy of the *Chicago Tribune*, popped it open to the front page, and froze in his tracks. Ten minutes later Big Ed walked into the office, raincoat collar turned up, water dripping. "Big Ed," Ferdie said, staring at him deadpan.

Big Ed stopped. A deadpan stare from Ferdie always preceded a catastrophe.

"Drop it on me," Big Ed said.

Ferdie guided him into his office, closed the door, ushered him to his side of the desk, helped him remove his coat, hung it in the corner, then walked back and helped Big Ed settle into his padded chair. He removed the morning *Tribune* from his coat pocket, carefully opened it, and laid it before Big Ed.

Dead center in the upper half of the front page was Walt's photograph of Gino and Hugo and the twenty-one others tumbling off the roof of the Badger bus into the Clearwater River. The three-inch headlines read, CHICAGO-BASED AFL-CIO UNION LOSING WAR IN THE WEST. Pages four through twelve had half of Walt's photographs and most of Louise's editorial. Big Ed's name appeared in the first line.

Big Ed leaped to his feet. He pounded his fist on the newspaper. The veins in his neck expanded and his eyes bugged. Ferdie stepped back, expecting something to explode. Big Ed began to turn gray, then blue. He tried to speak but put out only a muffled strangling sound. Ferdie quickly poured water from a silver decanter on the desk and handed the glass to Big Ed. Big Ed tried to swallow but couldn't, so Ferdie threw the water in his face. Big Ed gasped, and that released a torrent of words that backed Ferdie up three full steps.

Ferdie waited until Big Ed had to breath in, then quickly said, "You want I should make another unfair labor complaint and get down to Hughie at the NLR offices with it?"

"Fergit that," Big Ed shouted. "You get Hughie on the phone right now and tell him we're comin'." We'll make this complaint in person, and he's gonna have his mediators out there by tomorrow and they better get a mediation finished quick, or we go straight to the NLRB in Washington, D.C., and the United States Senate and the House of Representatives with this one. Now get movin'!"

A thousand miles further east, Mr. Hamilton Atwater hummed pleasantly in the bright morning sunshine that transformed the White House Rose Garden to a world of color and beauty. Slender, artistic, immaculate, he selected a beautiful pink rose, just opening, snipped it carefully with pruning shears, wrapped it tenderly in a moist paper towel, and walked through the tall French doors on the east wing of the White House. He paused to inspect his conservative navy blue suit, starched shirt, and deep wine tie in the full-length mirror beside the entrance to the oval room, then rapped lightly.

"Who's there?"

"It is I, Mr. President."

"Atwater? Well, come on in."

"Indeed," Atwater countered, and pushed the door open.

The round, bespectacled, bulldog face with the thinning hair on top raised from the pile of mail and newspapers on the large silver tray. Harry S. Truman studied Atwater for a moment.

"Something on your mind?"

"Oh, no, sir. Just the usual morning rose for your lapel."

Truman wrinkled his nose. "Just shove it in a vase somewhere. I don't know what bein' president has to do with wearin' roses."

"Very good, sir." Atwater disappeared for a moment while Truman continued plowing through the mail and newspapers methodically. He opened the *Post*, and the first word that caught his eye in the headline was "UNION." With a sour look on his face, he flattened the newspaper and began to read.

Five minutes later Atwater returned and placed the long-necked, cut-crystal vase on the corner of the great desk, turned it until it was precisely right, and stepped back to admire his work.

"Will there be anything else, sir?"

"Yeah. Get me some strong coffee."

Atwater raised a warning finger. "Naughty naughty," he said, smiling brilliantly. "You know what the doctors said."

"The doctors ain't here. Get the coffee."

"Very good, Mr. President."

Atwater returned two minutes later with a carafe of steaming coffee and a white milk china cup, and set the tray on the desk.

"Will there be anything else, Mr. President?"

"Not right now, but don't go far."

As Atwater quickly strode from the room and sat just outside the door, Truman poured coffee, sipped, smacked his lips at the heat, and tipped his head forward to concentrate on whatever it was the *Post* considered headline material about unions.

Two minutes later Atwater heard a chuckle through the closed door. One minute later, a muffled guffaw. A few seconds later, a wheezing laugh that swelled to an uproar. Atwater stood and rapped on the door.

"Is everything all right, Mr. President?"

The belly laugh continued unrestrained.

Atwater opened the door and hastened inside.

Truman was leaned back into his padded, overstuffed chair, tears running down his cheeks, fighting for air.

"What, may I ask, is so filled with mirth?" Atwater inquired.

Truman tried to speak but could not. He pointed at the newspaper and again succumbed to gales of laughter.

Atwater looked down at the newspaper, turned it partially to look, and his eyebrows arched. "Oh my goodness. Imagine that! Heh heh heh."

Truman leaned forward and by force of will caught his breath, took off his glasses and wiped them, then wiped his eyes and cheeks on his coat sleeve.

"Get J. Edgar."

"Yes, Mr. President."

Ten minutes later the stocky man with the jowls walked into the oval office.

"You wanted to see me, sir?"

"Yeah." Truman gestures and J. Edgar Hoover sits down.

"We just get those dad-blasted railroad unions whipped into line, and here we got some AFL-CIO idiots out there tryin' to cram unions down the throats of people who need a union like they need smallpox. Danged disgraceful. Hear about it?"

"Yes, sir."

"Hear how those folks handled it?"

"Only briefly."

Truman smiled, then chuckled. "Took enough guns off that union bunch to start a war, and . . ." Truman could not contain himself. He burst into laughter until it rang off the walls in the oval office in the White House. Two Secret Service agents came trotting. Maids and butlers and chefs stopped in their tracks, and turned to stare in the direction of the oval office.

J. Edgar sat impassively and waited.

Truman wheezed to a stop, then continued. "Made 'em throw all their weapons in the road, then loaded all twenty-three men in a 1928 Badger school bus, and ran the whole kit and kaboodle of 'em into the river."

He threw back his head and roared.

The Secret Service supervisor hit the red button.

The White House doctor burst into the oval office and instantly loosened Truman's tie and collar, peeled off his suit coat, and unbuttoned his long-sleeved shirt.

Truman regained enough control to blurt, "Hey, what do you think *you're* doin'?"

"Mr. President, you are having a seizure."

Truman shook his head. "Seizure baloney. I'm havin' the best laugh I've had in twenty years. You seen those

pictures? Look at them union boys, draggin' theirselves
out of the Clearwater River. And look at that choir,
standin' there drippin'. 'We Shall Gather at the River'! A
bear scarin' song."

He laughed so hard that his neck veins bulged and
sweat popped out on his round forehead.

"Here," the doctor said, "swallow this," and shoved a
pill at Truman. "It will relax you."

Truman pushed his hand away. "I don't need relaxin'.
I need about twenty more newspaper articles just like
that one." He sobered for a moment. "By thunder, you got
a problem, give it to a bunch of common folk. They'll
solve it, and they won't pussyfoot around doin' it, either."

He slowly brought himself under control. "Sure as
I'm sittin' here, the union's goin' to yell foul and demand
a hearing on an unfair labor practice charge. Then the
NLRB'll have to jump in the middle of it and spend
about ten million bucks of taxpayer money messin' up
what those folks out there have already fixed."

He stopped to collect his thoughts.

"J. Edgar, you get Eli. Send him out there right now
and tell him to stay undercover and keep an eye on what
happens. Let the locals handle this if they can, but if that
union bunch starts with rough stuff, like guns or something, I want to know it two minutes later. Tell Eli to
report direct to me two or three times a day until this
thing's over. You got that?"

"Yes, sir, I got that."

"Find out all you can about who took on the union
bunch and run 'em in the river." He burst into laughter
again. "Bear scarin' song! I ain't heard one like that since
I left Missouri!"

"Yes, sir. Anything else?"

"Not for now, but you check in with me personally every day." He turned to Atwater. "You get a call from J. Edgar, you run me down pronto and give it to me, no matter what I'm doin'."

"Yes, Mr. President."

"And get Bess and Margaret in here. They got to here this one."

Atwater strode quickly down the hall as it echoed with the sound of unrestrained laughter.

CHAPTER 9

"Homer, you awake down there?"

In the warmth of bright mid-morning sun, Tom Bradley dropped the nose of his airplane enough to line up with the dirt runway at the Lewiston airport and be certain nobody had left a pickup or the bulldozer parked on it.

"Tom, fer cryin' out loud," Homer exclaimed, "you bringin' the whole army air corps again?"

"Nope, just five this time. Someone from Chicago named Ziggman, and some guys with him. Most of 'em work for some government labor thing. Got a bunch of newfangled recording equipment and books and stuff. We're loaded heavy and comin' right on in."

"Watch the north end of the strip. We got us a mama badger out there in a burrow with a passel of babies, and she ain't about to move. We ain't got the heart to set baits or drown 'em out. Hole's about two feet wide and four feet deep, so watch sharp and don't hit it."

"Roger."

Bradley and his pilots put their planes down, dodged the badger hole, and stopped near the shack. Ten minutes later their passengers, luggage, and equipment stood in the dust of the high, arid plateau.

Homer walked out of the shack. "Mornin' gents, ma'am," he said pleasantly. "Welcome to Lewiston. I'm Homer. I tend the airstrip. Uh, someone supposed to meet you here?"

"Yah. I am Heinrich Ziggman. I am from the National Labor Relations Board of the United States of America. Zomeone was to be here for to pick us up."

Homer's jaw went slack at the rich German accent, and for a split second he studied Ziggman.

Heinrich Ziggman was corpulent, paunchy, perspiring, had a walrus mustache, blue eyes, short-cropped blond hair that defied comb or brush, and wore thick, gold-rimmed glasses. His jowls jiggled when he spoke. Born Peter Haufstad in Frankfurt, Germany, he had been inducted into the German Army in 1917, at age sixteen, to fight the French in World War I. His first day on the battlefield, a French mortar shell exploded 160 yards away. No one was hurt, but two minutes later Peter Haufstad was seen running eastward as hard as his thick legs would carry him, towards Frankfurt, with his sergeant chasing him, shaking his fist and shouting obscenities. But in a footrace a fast sergeant is no match for a scared private, and soon Peter was out of sight. He hid in a coal shed for six months, then one night snuck out, and six days later was in Switzerland, where he spent the next three years cleaning goat and cow stables for room and board, and began using the name Heinrich Ziggman, since Peter Haufstad was an army deserter.

After the war he hesitantly walked back to Frankfurt and got a job sweeping streets, until 1936 when Hitler organized his Nazi youth movement to develop the master race from the "pure Aryan" bloodline, which was easily identified in anyone who had blue eyes and blond hair. Ziggman was thirty-five years old, and not a youth, but when the brown-shirted Nazis saw his blue eyes and blond hair they didn't ask any questions, and he was shipped off in a railroad freight car to a mountain camp for training to rule the world. For two years the brown-shirts pounded him with training in brutality and dictatorial arrogance, and then in 1939 Hitler took Czechoslovakia and invaded Poland.

Ziggman knew all too well what was coming next, and once more walked to Switzerland at night, where he resumed work shovelling out cow and goat stalls. He remained in Switzerland until 1945, when he emigrated to England, then on to America, where he took a job in Washington, D. C., sweeping out the offices at the National Labor Relations Building. It was there he saw his first union mediation hearing, and he was enthralled beyond his wildest dreams by the dictatorial power vested in the mediator. The harsh training in the Nazi youth camp was not in vain! He swore upon his mother's picture he would one day be a mediator, and for the next year every waking moment was spent reading everything necessary to take the exam. He failed it twice, then passed, and beamed for ten days after they assigned him as an apprentice mediator.

He talked to himself in front of the mirror, trying to lose his decidedly German accent, and partially succeeded. Relaxed, he did reasonably well, but when he was stressed or excited he reverted to the language, and the style of Hitler's Germany and his youth camp training, and invariably launched off into discussions and topics that had nothing to do with unions or mediation hearings. Complaints were filed stating that when things got testy he would frequently lunge to his feet, shout *Achtung*, thrust out his lower lip, strut about with his hands on his hips, and browbeat the parties into cowed submission with words that included *himmel, donderhead,* and *gestupid.* His supervisor took a firm hand and told him that if he didn't mellow he would be reassigned to some position other than mediator. Ziggman struggled to control his dictatorial tendencies, and while he still had moments of relapse, the complaints lessened.

Inevitably, he was nicknamed Ziggy, which in his view was too close to Piggy, and he never ceased in his efforts to correct the derogation of his assumed name.

Homer looked at the others in the group, four men and a woman. "All of you with Mr. Ziggman?"

"Nein," said Ziggman. "Only these two men und Hilda. Hilda is the woman." He pointed to be certain Homer knew which one was Hilda.

Homer glanced at the remaining man. "You're not with Mr. Ziggman?"

The man shifted a badly chewed matchstick in his mouth to speak. His face was seamed and weathered, and he wore old, patched corduroy pants tucked into the top of scarred lace-up leather boots, a faded, blue-checkered shirt, an old, sweat-stained, shapeless gray felt hat, and broad suspenders. His seven-day beard stubble moved when he talked, and his Adam's apple bobbed.

"Naw, I just come to do a little prospectin' up north. Bought an old abandoned mine up there. I figger a case or two of dynamite in the right place might show some color."

The whine of a Ford automobile engine wound up to over 2,000 rpms interrupted, and they all turned to watch the county sheriff's car slowly crest the south edge of the plateau, followed by a second sedan. The cars stopped near the group of men and Clyde got out of one, Norman the other.

"Good morning," Clyde said in his best politician manner. "I'm Sheriff Clyde Milligan and this is Norman Quimby. Norman runs the newspaper. I was supposed to pick up some people from back east. Norman came to help. Is one of you Heinrich Ziggman?"

"Yah. Me," Ziggman said.

"Ready to go?"

"Yah."

"Clyde," Homer said, "you ought to have someone look at your Ford. That engine was sure wound up."

"Yeah," Clyde said, "can't get it out of low. Art's goin' to fix it next Monday."

They grunted and sweated to load the electronic equipment into Clyde's trunk and backseat, and one man climbed into the front seat. Clyde eyed the old mining prospector. "You got a way into town?"

The shaggy eyebrows raised in surprise. "Naw, I figgered to walk, like always."

"You intend staying around here until election?"

The suspendered shoulders shrugged. "Mebbe. If I hit color in the mine."

Clyde puckered while he considered if one more vote was worth it. It was. "I got space in the front seat if we squeeze. You're welcome to ride if you've a mind."

"Well, that's right neighborly. Reckon I will. I'll get a room at the Lumberjack, if it's still there."

Clyde drove the two men and the load of electronic recording equipment to the Lumberjack, while Norman drove Ziggman and the other two people to the Aloha, where Ziggman froze at the sight of the neon sign, which they kept lighted twenty-four hours of every day, year-round. For a moment he studied the swishing grass skirt.

"What kind of place is dis? We do not take rooms in places where girls wiggle und do things."

"That's just the sign. It doesn't mean anything. It's a good motel."

Ziggman eyed the ongoing construction. "They have not finished building dis place?" he asked.

"They had a fire, but you've got good rooms."

"Where will we meeting for the meditation?"

"The old high school."

"Old high school? No courthouse? No city hall or nothing?"

Norman shook his head. "Courthouse's got only one courtroom and we got a trial goin' there and Judge Hoffstader won't interrupt it. City hall's in the second story of Henry's hardware store, and he don't want all the traffic upstairs during business hours. The new high school roof leaked when it rained last April and they're tearing out the walls to replace the insulation and repaint."

"Where is da old high school?"

"East edge of town on Elm. Don't worry. I'll take you. When do you plan to start your mediation?"

"Nine o'clock in the morning. I must sending out notices today."

The old, one-room log high school was built at the edge of town in the wide-open spaces in 1890 and abandoned in 1932 when they built the new brick one at the other end of town. The black, rusted, potbellied stove still sat in the middle of the room, and the faded blackboard remained nailed to the wall. Four bullet holes graced the face of the old battered board, along with two long cuts where an axe blade and a hatchet had punched through in the midst of an intense and hotly discussed arithmetic lesson. After the school was abandoned, Lars Sodderquist let his milk cow graze in the school yard, and after several years, walking through the yard to the front door of the school was a study in stepping carefully where the cow had not.

In the early afternoon Hilda typed out the required notices to the parties involved in the mediation and attached copies of the six pages of charges Big Ed and Ferdie had listed. Ziggman signed them and handed them to Clyde to be served.

Clyde went to his office and reached for his phone.

"Number pleeuzz."

"Alice, get me Norman."

He waited.

"Norman, I've got official notices to be served on Abe and Beth. There's going to be an official United States NLRB hearing tomorrow at the old high school, with electricity and all, and Abe and Beth got to be served with these notices. You got to do it."

Alice's eyes bugged.

Norman said, "Why me?"

"Because my Ford won't make that run again in low gear. I'll serve the union guys at the hotel and motel, but you got to go out to Abe and Beth. Now get on over here."

Clyde hung up and Alice's hands flew as she jammed three plugs into her switchboard. "Louise, Phoebe, Clara, sit down! This here's serious!"

Clyde gave copies of the notice to Norman, and then delivered copies to Gino and Hugo. Then Clyde drove Ziggman to the dilapidated old high school to set up his recording equipment. Ziggman took one look at the school and his lip curled. Then his eyes dropped to the yard, and he stopped.

"We must remove da green cow schtuff," he said loudly. "We cannot conduct mediation hearings in da middle of green cow schtuff."

Clyde scratched under his chin as he studied the yard. "That'll take about three days, and two men with pitchforks and a pickup truck," he said. "Want to wait?"

Ziggman looked disgusted. "We cannot wait. We must clearing away da green schtuff from da door."

"I'll send someone out," Clyde said. "Anything else?"

"Yah. Where is da power with electricity? We must recording da entire mediation proceeding on the recording machines and that will require electricity."

"We never had electricity out here before, but I'll get Duke from city maintenance to run a line out here special."

"Yah, you do that."

Ziggman tiptoed through the yard to the front door and pushed it open on rusted hinges that complained. He looked at the dusty, cobwebbed interior of the ancient structure and shook his head in disbelief. "We will needing chairs and a large table at the front, and the cobwebs and dust is to go." He spied the scarred blackboard and both eyebrows arched. "Bullet holes? What kind of school was this?"

"Regular high school. Those lumberjacks' kids were pretty rough back in the 1890s."

"We remove da blackboard," Ziggman insisted.

In the late afternoon, Duke and Elmer tapped into the nearest power line and strung a cable to the old schoolhouse roof, down the stovepipe, out the stove door to the front of the room, and connected a six-plug outlet. Meanwhile, Dennis and Waldo from the school district dusted and swept the room, replaced desks and the old table with benches and a larger table, and pulled the faded blackboard from the wall. Then they used lawn rakes to clear a six-foot-wide path in the yard, through the green cow stuff. The path was bordered by berms of the rich fertilizer, eighteen inches high.

Twenty-eight miles east, in Hollis, with the sun touching the western rim, and the Clearwater glowing like something alive, Norman stopped his sedan in front of Abe's home. Abe and Beth walked out onto the front porch.

"Howdy, Norman. Just in time for supper. Come on in and set."

"Thanks anyways, but I can't. I got to get back to town. Clyde sent me out to give you these notices. Looks like there's goin' to be a mediation in town in the morning. A bunch of government people flew in today and it looks official. You're supposed to be there."

"A mediation for what?"

"Here's your official notice. The charges are listed there."

Norman handed the notice to Abe, who looked at the large, black, ominous letters, NLRB at the top, and scanned the first page.

"Old high school at nine o'clock?"

"Looks that way."

Abe looked at Beth, then back at Norman. "Just me?"

"Whoever he has on the notice."

Abe shrugged. "Okay. We'll be there. How many did the NLRB send?"

"Four."

Norman turned at the sound of a pickup truck behind, and Guy and Emma Feeney pulled to a stop.

"Seen Norman come by and figgered somethin' might be wrong," Guy exclaimed. "You okay, Abe?"

"Yeah. Norman just brought out some official notices. Looks like we got an NLRB mediation hearing tomorrow in town at the old high school."

Guy's jaw dropped open. "What's this all about?" He looked at Norman.

Norman shook his head. "I don't know any more than what the notice says."

Guy rubbed the back of his neck. "If that don't beat all."

Norman turned. "I got to get back to town. Don't be late."

"Hey," Abe said, "stop by Elbert's place and tell him I'll be gone tomorrow. Him and Jack are comin' in to help hang Mattie's pork in the smokehouse. Tell Elbert to go ahead and do it without me. He knows what to do."

"Okay. I'll tell him."

Norman pulled out and Abe looked at Guy and Emma. "Had supper? Come on. We're just sittin' down."

Five minutes later Abe said grace, and in the same breath, "Pass the spuds."

Guy said, "What's in that notice?"

Abe tossed it beside Guy's plate and Guy studied the first two pages. His eyes grew large and round as he continued. Finally he laid the paperwork on the tabletop and looked solemnly at Abe.

"Abe, take my pickup and make a run for Canada. If them NLRB guys believe half of that, you'll be in jail for about two hundred years."

Abe poured steaming brown gravy over his mound of fluffy, mashed potatoes. "Looks like this oughta be a real hummer."

CHAPTER 10

"Good mornin' all you good folks out there, this is Lou Gibney as usual broadscattering sunshine and joy all up and down the Clearwater."

He turned down the microphone and let the turntable spin and waited while "The Star-Spangled Banner" reached out through the airwaves, over the mountains and valleys and the river.

"Today's the day we start the NLRB mediation hearing between the union and Abe and Beth Jones's meat plant up at Hollis. We got a little bit of everything involved in this one, including about twenty-three visitors from Chicago who came with more guns than the U.S. Marines, and about six pages of charges against Abe and Beth that include everything except divorce. Might want to grab a sandwich and visit us at the old Lewiston High School."

By eight o'clock pickup trucks were rolling through town and stopping at the old ramshackle schoolhouse. By nine o'clock they were parking four blocks away.

Henrich Ziggman fidgeted with his pocket watch, then cleared his throat and spoke to Hilda Schwartz, his clerk, seated beside him. He was already nervous and excited, and Hilda took a firm grip on herself, preparing for what she knew was coming.

Ziggman licked his lips and nervously jammed his pocket watch back into his vest pocket. "It is nine o'clocken A.M. in da morning and time to start this meeting." He pushed his gold-rimmed glasses back up his nose and rose to his feet. The blank wall where the old blackboard had hung was behind him, the table in front.

"Ladies and gentlemen, my name is Henrich Ziggman. Not Ziggy. The reason I tell you this is that Ziggy sounds just like Piggy when you say it too fast and I do not like being called Piggy. So I telling you mine name is Ziggman. Mine father was . . ."

Hilda pulled on his coat sleeve and he looked down at her and she whispered loudly, "Start the mediation."

He cleared his throat officiously and looked stern. "I will telling you about mine father later, when is a better time. I was sent here to this place by the Nazi Labor Relations Board in Washington, D.C., to conduct a mediation meeting to hearing evidence about unfair labor schtuff."

Everyone in the room gasped and Hilda jerked his coattail violently and hissed "*National* Labor Relations Board. Not *Nazi! National!*"

Louise Quimby jerked erect and her eyes bugged as she scribbled on her pad, "The Nazi Labor Relations Board!"

Ziggman licked suddenly dry lips and scanned the sea of thin-lipped faces and dead eyes that were boring holes through him. "Did I saying Nazi? Obviously if I said Nazi it was a mistaken error. The Nazis is not got noddink with this to do. The Nazis was in Germany as you all know. Berlin and Frankfurt and Munich and Stuttgart and other places like that. Germany is a long ways from here, far past Connecticut and Vermont." He straightened his spine and squared his shoulders. "I remember when I was younger in Germany, the Nazis came marching in the streets in the brown shirts and black boots and they scare the holy wienerschnitzel out of us. They is not in Washington, D.C., and they did not send me here. In Washington, D.C., is this big building with . . ."

"Start the mediation," came Hilda's hiss.

Plump and blond, Hilda sat at his left elbow with a microphone on a base, a notepad, and four yellow, sharpened, number two pencils at her fingertips. Hilda had been carefully coached to do two things: listen intently to every word Ziggman spoke and correct him when he made mistakes, and faithfully see to it that he followed standard mediation hearing procedures.

In the corner behind Ziggman and Hilda, Paul Huff and Hans Wasserman managed the electronic recording equipment, eyes glued on Ziggman, ready to instantly shut down everything when Ziggman made mistakes. All too often the translators back in the offices in Washington, D.C., who had to transcribe the recordings of Ziggman's mediation meetings, had developed serious muscle twitches in their faces and hands that wouldn't go away for weeks. One wrote to the Secretary of Labor begging for a transfer after spending nine hours trying to translate "gehalten, dumpkoff," and "droppenhead." The transfer was not granted, but the next day Hilda, Paul, and Hans were called into a closed meeting and spent six hours formulating a plan to eliminate any further such things.

Past Hilda, on Ziggman's left, Gino and Hugo sat dressed in their pin-stripe suits, staring deadpan out over the audience. To Ziggman's right sat Abe and Beth. Beth looked embarrassed, and Abe moved his feet back and forth nervously.

In front of the table, facing Ziggman, Tiny sat on the end of the first bench, with the other twenty members of the union negotiation team next to him, all silent, suits immaculate, hair parted in the middle and plastered down, facial expressions angelic, like choir boys. Behind them, every bench, every corner of the room was jammed. A faint odor rose from green splotches on the floor that had been tracked in by those who had ignored it as they walked through the yard, or were less nimble in their footwork. Pickup trucks and cars and a few farm wagons and buggies were crowded around the building, two hundred yards in every direction.

Sprawled on a chair just inside the door was the old mining prospector that had arrived on the airplane with Ziggman. He was chewing on a long blade of cheat grass. His ancient, icy gray eyes moved about the room slowly, missing nothing, no one. Louise Quimby sat near the front, pencil and pad in hand to take notes for the newspaper. The door and windows were open, and people stood quietly outside, listening.

Ziggman continued. "I have before me in mine hand a list of unfair labor charges brought by the AFL-CIO union against the Clearwater Meat Company which is located in the town of Hollis, Iowa, and is owned by Abe Jones and his wife."

Abe glanced at Ziggman, and someone in the audience called out, "Idaho, not Iowa."

Ziggman's mouth puckered and he looked at Hilda, and she nodded vigorously. "Idaho." Ziggman brought the paper close to his face. "That is correct. Idaho. Not

Iowa. Iowa is not here. Iowa is out by Florida. Hilda will correct the record." For a moment Ziggman looked judicial, to distract from the error.

"For the record, I must ask each party if they have received and read a copy of the charges and did you understand the charges, and do you wish to proceed with this hearing at this time?"

"Yes," sighed Abe.

"Yeah," answered Gino.

"That is good. I shall now reading all of the charges."

Abe groaned. "All six pages? That'll take about an hour. Can't we move on?"

"Do you waiving the reading of the charges?"

There was a titter of laughter that died quickly.

Abe said, "Yes, I'm waiving it."

"What do you say about dese charges? Is they true or is they false?"

Abe's face darkened. "They're false."

Ziggman turned to Gino. "You have heard that dese charges is a fib. Do you wish to stop now or go on?"

"Like, go on. Sure."

"Very well. We shall taking evidence on the first charge." Ziggman officiously smoothed the paper and read, "Obstructing of union negotiators who are doing whatever it is union negotiators do when they do union business." He paused and pursed his mouth for a moment, then looked at Gino. "Who will giving evidence of this charge?"

Gino stood. "Me, your honor."

"Ah! Good. You see, taking the evidence is necessary." His eyes shined as he looked out over his audience. "In other countries, they don't taking evidence. They just taking the list of all the bad things and they take the bad guys out in back behind the building and they find a wall, and they line up the bad guys and they march out the soldiers with the bullets and," he shrugged, "bambambambam. No more bad guys, no more negotiations, no more nothing."

A murmur from the audience snapped him from his reverie and he cleared his throat and tried to determine in his mind where he was in the proceeding.

Louise was scribbling wildly on her pad.

"But that is not how we do it here!" His fist thumped on the table. "This is the U.S. of America. Here we taking evidence *first*, and *then* vil go out in back and find a wall and . . ."

Hilda jerked violently on his sleeve and whispered desperately, "Have the witnesses sworn in."

"Oh! Ja! Did I forgetting that?" He forced a nervous laugh. "Swearing in the witnesses. All the witnesses who will giving evidence stand now on your feet and raise the hand."

"The *right* hand," Hilda whispered hoarsely.

He looked down at her frightened eyes. "Mine right hand you say? Is something with my right hand wrong?" He looked at his right hand.

"Tell the witnesses to raise their right hands!"

"Ja. Oh, ja. Witnesses vil raising their right handers."

All twenty-three men in their pin-stripe suits stood and faced Ziggman.

"Hilda vil schwearing the witnesses," Ziggman said proudly, and turned slightly towards her. "You see, Hilda is mine assistant. She also is from Germany. Stuttgart. Stuttgart is a wonderful place, with flowers and beer and frauleins. Once I was in Stuttgart and there was this fraulein and I . . ."

Hilda jerked to her feet and Ziggman's eyebrows raised in question. "Is someding wrong? You was not the fraulein in . . ."

Hilda ignored him and turned to Gino. "All raise your right hands to be sworn as witnesses."

They all raised their hands and were sworn to tell the truth.

Ziggman's face sobered. His brow furrowed and he looked fierce. "We are now goink to take the evidences. That is the most important part. You will all telling the truth. If you telling a fib, we call Washington, D.C., and they send out the FIB and they—"

Hilda grabbed his sleeve and he stopped and looked down. "We must giving the warning about what we do if they tell fibs."

"It's the FBI, not the FIB."

Ziggman froze for a moment while he sorted it out, then raised his head. "Did I saying FIB? That is an incorrect error. They send out the FBI and they come with badges and pistols and take you away. So don't telling no fibs."

He looked down at Hilda for approval and she sighed wearily, and he nodded and stopped for a moment to determine what came next. He turned to Gino.

"So, you will giving the first evidence. Telling us what they did that is an unfair labor practice."

Gino nodded "Yeah, right, well, see, our union—AFL-CIO—wrote a letter to Clearwater Meat Company like we're supposed to, sayin' we want to come negotiate about gettin' the union in. So Bid Ed . . . excuse me, the

154

president of the union sent us to do the talkin'. So on that day, there we was, seven of us drivin' the hearse down this road out to Hollis to talk to—"

Ziggman suddenly raised his hand in alarm. "Hearse? Who was dead? This is not the place where they tried killing you. That comes later."

There were gasps everywhere, and Louise half rose from her chair, her pencil racing through page after page of her pad. The old miner by the rear door grinned and shifted the shaft of cheat grass from one side of his mouth to the other.

Gino paused for a moment. "Naw, you got it wrong. We was drivin' a hearse because the road was washed out and the Greyhound bus couldn't make it, so we went to rent a limo, but they don't rent limos in Boise, so, like, this guy made us this deal. He'd sell us . . ."

Ziggman's hand shot up again. "I do not understanding about the bus and the hearse. What has a hearse with this charge to do?"

"Yer honor," Gino exclaimed, "the hearse ain't got nothin' to do with no charge. You asked so I was tellin', we bought the hearse in Boise to make the trip to Lewiston. We was drivin' the hearse."

"Without nobody being dead?"

"Yeah. There wasn't nobody dead. It was an old one. We bought it from a used car dealer in Boise. See, he made us a deal . . ."

Ziggman's hand went up. "So you drove in the hearse without nobody being dead, to Hollis. Is that correct?"

"Yeah," beamed Gino. "Like, now you got it."

Ziggman nodded his head broadly, pride showing. "Thank you. Go on with the evidences."

Gino launched into it again. "So there we was drivin' peacefully to Hollis, when all of a sudden about twenty pickup trucks come whippin' down the road directly at us, at high speed, so naturally we stopped."

Gino paused for dramatic effect. Ziggman's face puckered with intensity. His eyes narrowed and his breathing slowed. "Yah," he said, "go on. And then what happened?"

Gino squared his shoulders and looked brave. "I got out and I asked these guys, I says, nice day we're havin', and I says, we're lookin' for the Clearwater Meat Company on account of we was sent to talk about a union, and if youse guys could tell us where it is at, we would be thankful." He smiled humbly.

Ziggman relaxed with a broad smile. "And what did they do?"

Gino's hand thumped the table and his sides heaved as he delivered his speech. "Like, them guys got out of their trucks, maybe forty of 'em, and they had shotguns and pistols, and they started over towards us. We was parked there, peaceful, and Dom tries to open the back door to get out to beg for mercy, see, and one of them guys whips up his shotgun and blasts the window clean out of the door."

Ziggman jerked erect, flames suddenly leaping from his eyes. "Heavens!" he blurted. "Bam! Just like that and the window is kaput?"

Gino took a deep breath and locked frightened eyes with Ziggman. "Bam! Gone! Just like that! So we hollered we didn't want no trouble, and they said, well, you're going to get it, and then they jumped on us, all of 'em, with billy clubs and chains and baseball bats and like that."

He paused and glanced at the audience, who sat wide-eyed in stunned fascination. "We gave 'em a battle, swingin' and standin' up for ourselves, just seven of us against forty of them. We fought for oh, probably about an hour before they got tired and jumped back in their trucks and drove back where they come from."

No one in the room stirred in the breathless silence.

Gino stopped and shook his head sadly and then settled his face forward until his chin was on his chest. "Poor Dom. Poor Tony. There they was, subconscious on the ground from all their wounds. It was only by the hand of Providence that they was spared. We got 'em to the hospital in time."

Abe and Beth, eyebrows arched in astonishment, were staring at Gino. Louise was scribbling notes eight pages a minute. The old miner had his head down, shoulders shaking in silent laughter. Murmuring broke out in the room, and it rose to a crescendo as everyone spoke at once. "That's a pack of lies. Nobody up at Hollis would do that. Abe and Beth? That's crazy!"

Ziggman stood and sucked in his chin and threw out his chest. "Achtung," he barked. "We are taking evidence. You will stopping the noise or we will calling the FIB and that will be the end of that!"

The room quieted and Ziggman turned back to Gino. "Do you knowing who was dese men who hitted your bodies and shooted your hearse?"

"Yeah, like, their main guy was Elbert. We learnt that later. Elbert Pike."

"What has Elbow Piker with Abe Jones to do?"

Hilda grabbed his arm. "Elbert Pike. Not Elbow Piker."

Ziggman looked baffled. "Elbow? Did I saying Elbow? The elbow is part of the arm what makes you lift beer steins and . . ." He sobered and raised his head. "Elbert Piker, not elbow."

"He's the main guy who works for Abe Jones."

Ziggman inhaled deeply and bristled with importance as he summarized. "So you come to discussing a union with the Abe Jones company and they sending forty men who put assaults on your bodies and shots on your hearse. Is that correct?"

Gino solemnly nodded his head. "That is correct."

"Was Mr. Abe Jones one of those men?"

"No, but he sent 'em. They was his reg'lar employees."

Ziggman slowly turned accusatory eyes at Abe, who looked startled. Then Ziggman turned back to Gino. "Was there any others who saw dese forty men put the assaults and shots on you?"

"None I know of. It was just us and them. But we got proof. We got the hearse right out there beside the building, with the window blowed out!" Gino raised his arm, pointing.

Ziggman nodded his head solemnly. "Everybody will don't move until I am returning from to inspect the window which is kaput!"

He strode from the room and picked his way through the green stuff to the hearse, and with narrowed eyes examined the shattered window and the few buckshot pits in the door and frame before he marched stoically back to his place at the head of the table.

He spoke to Hilda. "The record will show that the window of the hearse is kaput by a shotgun."

He sat down and turned gravely to Gino. "Have you telling us all the evidences you got?"

"Yes sir, on the first charge of assault, but I got a lot more to say later about all them other charges."

Ziggman nodded. "We will talking about the other charges later. Do you have more who vil witnessing about this charge?"

"Yes, your honor, that we do."

Tony, Dom, Franco, Augie, Guiseppe, and finally Vinnie, were sworn and recited the story verbatim as Gino had done, while Ziggman listened with rapt attention, and Hilda and Paul and Hans worked intently to be certain they marked the places where corrections were needed.

Ziggman pulled out his large pocket watch. "The clock is noon. We vil stop for lunch and continue at half past one-thirty P.M."

Instantly the room was filled with talk as people filtered outside to stand in groups exclaiming about the sensational revelations of the morning.

Louise ran to the nearest phone.

"Number pleeuzz."

"Alice, get Norman at the office, and then get Clara and Phoebe on the line and listen to this. This is just absolutely unbelievable—the biggest story since VJ Day when the Japanese surrendered."

Norman picked up the phone on the first ring and Louise spoke before he did. "Norman, grab a pencil, and if you ever did anything right in your life, get this one right. We've got Nazis and assault and shooting and attempted murder so far, and it's just started. Now start writing while I talk."

For twenty minutes she dictated from her notes while Norman scribbled and Alice and Clara and Phoebe gasped, and then she concluded. "Norman, you get all that typeset right now, and I'll call again the second we finish. This'll be a special edition for sure. Get hold of Lou Gibney and make a deal. Alice, do you and Phoebe and Clara understand how big this is?"

"Oh, definitely!"

"You know what to do?"

"Of course. Certainly."

"Okay. I've got to go back. Do your duty."

At 1:30 P.M. Ziggman shuffled his papers and looked once again at the sea of intense, expectant faces.

"We shall now take evidence on the second unfair charge, which is attempted murder on the bodies of union negotiators in the course of while they were doing their duty." He turned to Abe. "Did you doing an attempted murder?"

Abe leaned forward. "Attempted murder? On who? I don't know what you're talking about."

Ziggman looked at Gino, who was now seated next to Hugo, facing Ziggman. "Who do you wish to giving evidences on this charge?"

Gino turned in his chair and pointed. "It was Hugo they tried to murder. He will give evidence."

Hugo was sworn, and cleared his throat. His low, gravelly voice boomed. "When Big Ed . . . er . . . the president of this here union heard about the assaults on the persons of Gino and the others he says we must do our American duty and assist our brothers in the union.

So at great expense he sent me and Tiny and the others here on the front benches out here and he gave us special instructions, see."

Hugo paused and closed his eyes and screwed his face into a prune as he labored to remember every word.

"He says, Hugo, he says, our brothers out there in the west is in trouble and they was assaulted. Youse get Tiny and a few of our other men who ain't involved in buildin' the new orphanage, or helpin' Father Flanagan coach the Little League baseball team, and youse guys get on an airplane and go out into those mountains and help spread peace and goodwill."

Hugo paused and looked proud at how he had delivered the first part of his speech, then took a deep breath and moved on.

"So me and Tiny searched and found fourteen other guys that wasn't helpin' at the orphanage or coachin' baseball, and we come here to Lewiston, Idaho. We brung along new artillery for Gino and the boys and . . ."

Suddenly his mouth rounded and he uttered a muffled "OOOOO," and looked at Gino, pained. He leaned slightly to his right and whispered hoarsely, "Now what for didja go and whomp on my foot under the table?"

Gino shoved his mouth close to Hugo's ear and gritted out, "Don't tell 'em about the artillery, stupid!"

Ziggman held up his hand. "Did I hearing the word *artillery*? What is artillery to do with this? Did you brinking cannon and mortars and like dat?"

Hugo swallowed and turned back to Ziggman. "Gino has reminded me that I have incorrectly used a woid by mistake. See, the orphans and the nuns at the convent back in Chicago, from whence we are come forth, they

161

read to us out of the Good Book all them good preambles, and they call 'em the church's artillery. So what I meant was, when me and Tiny and the others come out here to help, we brung Bibles. At least a dozen or two. That there's the artillery."

Hugo grinned broadly at his inspired recovery.

Ziggman scratched his head. "Preambles? Explain preambles."

Gino leaned over. "Parables, stupid."

Hugo's eyebrows raised, and he stammered, "These here preambles is a lot like parables."

Ziggman looked confused. "So, go on."

Hugo sighed with relief. "So when we got here we read some of them preambles and decided we oughta forgive them gorillas what put the assault and the shots on Gino and his guys. But we couldn't find no way to get out there, so we had to buy this old bus to make the trip. Then we loads up all the artillery . . . OOOO . . ." he glowered at Gino again, "and then we starts drivin' out this country road so's we could find them guys, and there we was, drivin' along and singin' hallelujahs, when all of a sudden outta nowhere, here come them guys again. Fifty or sixty of 'em. They stopped the bus and started shoutin' and wavin' their artillery and tellin' us to get out of the bus or they was goin' to set it on fire."

Ziggman reared straight up. "They was waving Bibles?"

Hugo winced and for a moment his face puckered. "Well, no, they was wavin' *their* artillery, which was pistols and shotguns. *Our* artillery was Bibles."

Ziggman's head bobbed. "So they had artillery and you had Bibles and they was going to burn the bus?"

Hugo took his cue perfectly. "Oh yeah, absolutely, for certain. The bus and all of us inside."

"So, what did you do?"

"Well, we done what them preambles taught us to do. We raised our hands and come out of the bus one at a time, shoutin' hallelujahs. That's what we done. Yessir, that's exactly what we done."

"And then what happened?"

"Why, right away they put assaults all over us. They beat us with baseball bats and billy clubs and stuff. Poor Tiny, and me, and half the others, they rendered subconscious right there on the road." Hugo was warming up to his story. "And they kept on kickin' on us, and then they made the others drag us back into the bus, subconscious and bleedin' and all, and they threatened to shoot everybody with them shotguns if the others didn't all stand in the back of the bus. So our guys all done what they was told, because that's what them preambles teaches."

Hugo paused to gather his thoughts.

Ziggman waited anxiously.

Abe looked at Beth in wondering awe.

Hugo rose from the table and stood with feet braced. "And then their main bozo, whose name I did not know until later—Elbert Pike—sits down in the driver's seat of our bus and right then we knowed he meant to kill us all. Yessir, we knowed it."

He drew a deep breath. "But the Good Book says, turn the other cheek, so we turned it. We hollered and told him we forgave him for what he was about to do and we shouted praises, and what he done then, he started the bus, and he turned it, and he aimed it right smack-dab at the river."

163

Ziggman gasped. The audience tittered. Abe chuckled outright. Clyde choked trying to contain himself. The old miner near the door jammed a hand over his mouth and his shoulders shook for several seconds.

"Yessir, I remember it like doomsday. Him steerin' that old bus down towards the deep, cold river, bouncin' around, and him laughin' and singin' the whole time like he was crazy or somethin'."

Ziggman raised a hand. "Just a moment. You was subconscious in the front of the bus. Yah? How did you knowing that bus was going to doomsday?"

Hugo blanched and swallowed hard. "Tiny told me later."

Ziggman shook his head. "Tiny was subconscious with you. How did he know?"

Hugo shrugged. "Someone told him later."

Ziggman shook his head.

Hugo continued. "Let me finish. Let me see, where was I?" He looked at Gino. "What was the next line?"

Gino leaned over. "The water dimwit. You hit the water."

Hugo nodded. "Yeah. Right." He straightened and looked at Ziggman. "Then we hit the cold water and we went into the deepest part. It come right on in the bus, and we was trapped, and we knew we was all goin' to drown. And we would of, except we got out the windows and climbed on the top. And there we was, callin' out for help, and them assault guys was wavin' their guns and yellin' they'd shoot if we tried to get out of the river."

White-faced, Ziggman blurted, "You was trapped in the cold water?"

"Yes, your honor, we was trapped! Then a monster wave rolled the bus on over and threw us in the water, and we all stared to drown. Yessir, right there in front of those men with the guns, and they was jumpin' up and down laughin'."

He drew and released a great breath. "But again the hand of Providence saved us. We was guided to a shallow place and we fought and battled to the bank, and there we lay, near death, all of us."

Ziggman was holding his breath.

"But we lived!" Hugo exclaimed.

Ziggman exhaled. "Heaven be praised!"

"So them guys jabs us with them shotguns and makes us stand, and we knowed they was goin' to start shootin', so we stood there shoulder to shoulder and we starts singin' hymns and hallelujahs again. And the hearts of those assault gorillas were softened, and we walked up the road, singin', and walked clean back to Lewiston."

Hugo's forehead wrinkled while he tried to remember if he had said all his lines, and, satisfied, he sat down.

Ziggman sighed heavily. "So you was rescued when you had a miracle. Marvelous." Suddenly remembering he was conducting a mediation, he sobered. "Someone else is going to give evidence on this charge?"

"Yeah. Tiny."

Tiny rose to his full seven feet and Ziggman's eyes popped, and brief mutterings were heard from the audience. Tiny was sworn as a witness, and Ziggman turned to him. "What evidence are you giving?" he asked.

Tiny's ponderous face clouded for a minute while he tried to remember. "Like Hugo said. They beat us up and tried to drown us." He glanced at Gino to see if he had done it right, and Gino hissed, "The shotguns!"

"Oh yeah. They had shotguns." He glanced at Gino again, and Gino mouthed the words *baseball bats*.

"An' baseball bats." He shrugged and didn't look at Gino again.

"Did they assaulted you with baseball bats and clubs and shotguns?"

"Yeah. Right."

"Was you rendered subconscious?"

"Yeah. Somethin' hit me."

"What?"

"A truck, maybe."

Laughter tittered and died.

Ziggman looked righteous. "Did you singing hymns and hallelujahs?"

Tiny's face puckered and he licked dry lips and leaned over to Gino and whispered, "What's with this hymns and hallelujahs. I don't remember—"

Gino winced and cut in. "Just say yes, you idiot."

Tiny straightened. "Yeah. We done that."

"Good," said Ziggman. "And was the main bad man named Piker?"

"Uh, yeah. Piker. I learnt that later."

"And Piker is working for Abe Jones's meat company?"

Tiny shrugged. "Yeah. Sure."

Ziggman shook his head and made notes. "Someone else is going to give evidence?"

One by one, as the afternoon wore on, each of the men who had stepped out the bus door to face Elbert and had fallen to his sledgehammer fists were sworn, and they began taking turns repeating the story already given by Hugo and Tiny, each adding an embellishment here and there.

At three o'clock P.M. the old miner quietly slipped out the back door, climbed into the clattery old junker Chevy pickup he had bought for $37.00 from Harley's Used Car Corral, and drove to Elmer's hardware store, four doors up from the newspaper office. He bought a small hand drill and a one-half inch drillbit, twelve inches long, then drove to the Lumberjack and walked down the hall to Gino's room. He drew a ring of half-dozen keys from his trouser pocket, selected one, looked up and down the hall, and quickly opened Gino's door. Inside, he located eighteen pistols and six submachine guns in twenty seconds, then walked to the east wall and removed a faded painting of Sacajawea, the Shoshone Indian girl who had been the guide for Lewis and Clark. Quickly he drilled a one-half-inch hole through the wall and cleaned up the wood curls. He forced two wires connected to a miniature microphone through the hole, lodged the small microphone at the hole entrance, replaced Sacajawea, glanced around the cluttered room to be sure no one could tell he had been there, and walked out.

He entered his own room next door, laid the drill and drillbit on his bed, and walked to the wall. In less than a minute he had the two wires connected to a small, battery-powered speaker, plugged into a headset, tested it to be certain it was working, and then walked back into the street to the dilapidated old pickup. Ten minutes later he was back at the old schoolhouse, once again lounging on his chair, leaned back against the back wall, chewing a fresh sprig of cheat grass while Gino's squad continued to testify.

At 4:35 the last witness finished, glanced at Gino for approval, and sat down.

Ziggman pulled out his pocket watch. "It is now 4:35. We will stop for today and start again at clocken 9:00 A.M. in da mornink."

The room instantly filled with the sounds of chairs and benches moving and a rush of people's voices. Hilda and Hans and Paul exhaled weary breaths and their shoulders slumped. Louise Quimby was out the door like a cannon shot.

The old miner stood and stretched and spat out the mangled stem of cheat grass, and walked out into the warm, bright June sunshine rich with the aroma of green cow stuff.

At 5:15 P.M. the miner was hunched over a small table in his room at the Lumberjack, headset clamped to his head while he listened intently to Gino giving orders to the other twenty-two men standing silently in the room. Twice a grin twitched the corners of the miner's mouth, and he murmured quietly, "So that's their plan."

At six o'clock Gino's room emptied; and the miner took the headset from his ears and leaned back in his chair and blew air, thinking. Then for fifteen minutes he wrote thoughtfully with a blunt pencil on a yellow pad, signed it "A Friend," inserted the folded message in his shirt pocket, and walked back into the street.

At six-twenty, in the splendor of reds and yellows of a sun disappearing behind the western rim of the Sawtooth Mountains, he wandered past the newspaper office and slowed while his jaw worked on a matchstick.

Inside he recognized Abe, Beth, Buster, Alice, Phoebe, Clara, Louise, Norman, Clyde, Walt, Lou Gibney, and Guy Feeney; and there were at least twenty other persons unknown to him, all of them excited, pointing, exclaiming. Silently he slipped the yellow message through the mail slot in the door and continued on, unnoticed, across the street to wait and watch.

Two minutes later Alice stopped in her tracks and walked to the door, where she stooped over and picked up the message. Quickly she scanned it, clapped her hand over her mouth, spun, and barged through the crowd to thrust the paper at Louise. Louise read it, her eyes popped, and instantly she leaped to the top of Norman's desk and shouted the crowd into silence. She read the message aloud, climbed down from the desk, and for the next fifteen minutes bedlam ruled supreme as everyone emphatically made their contribution to a plan.

Louise once again mounted the desk and recited what they had agreed to. Everyone nodded vigorously, and then the old miner saw her lips form the words, "Okay, let's go," and they bolted for the door. He leaned casually against the wall across the street, cleaning his fingernails with a pocketknife as they boiled out of the newspaper office and each ran for their pickup trucks, half Fords, half Chevys.

At six-fifty he drove his old junker across the river to Clarkston to the town gas station, where he found a public phone. He lifted the earpiece and waited. "Number pleeuzz."

"Operator, is this the phone on the Lewiston exchange?"

"No sir. This is Clarkston, Washington."

"Good. I have a long-distance call to make. Washington, D.C., to Harry. The number is 1-0-0-0."

"Sir, it's after ten o'clock in Washington, D.C."

"I know. Harry'll take the call."

The circuits clicked, the phone rang twice, and a blunt, nasal voice twanged. "Harry here. Who's calling this time of night?"

"Harry, Eli. You in bed?"

"Eli! Of course I'm in bed. I been worried about you. You all right?"

"Fine. There's some things I thought you should know."

"Let's have it."

"We finished the first day of mediation testimony on the first two charges against the local meat company. Assault and attempted murder."

"*What?* What's goin' on? A criminal trial?"

"To hear these union witnesses tell it, they're all welfare workers out here to spread peace and goodwill among the locals. They got beat up twice, dumped in the river once, robbed, and shot at."

A soft chuckle came over the line.

"Harry, the average height of these guys is about six foot eight, and the average weight is around three seventy. I think their collective IQ is close to the shoe size of the biggest one, and that's around eighteen."

Eli paused for the guffaw.

"The truth is, these goons went out to intimidate just about everybody in Hollis, where Abe Jones runs his little meat company, and they ran into the wrong guy. They peeved Elbert Pike."

"Who's Elbert Pike?"

"Just one of the men who works intermittently for Abe Jones."

"Big fella?"

"No. About five feet ten, but strong from the hips up, and rumor has it there's nobody within five hundred miles who can hit harder with his fists. He put six of these goons down in three minutes."

Uproarious laughter interrupted for twenty seconds, then quieted. "Dang, I wish I'd'a seen that. Go on."

"I listened on a hidden wire to the union guys make their plan after the mediation. They know if the bunch from Hollis shows up tomorrow and tells the truth, the union's going to be in trouble. So they plan to send about sixteen of their goons out to stop the people coming in from Hollis."

"Sixteen? How are they getting out to Hollis?"

"They bought a used cattle truck."

"A what?"

"A beat-up old cattle truck with dried green stuff all over. There was nothing else in Lewiston big enough for all of 'em."

A belly laugh stopped everything for thirty seconds, and then Harry settled down. "Eli, I'm comin' out there. I just gotta see this."

"You better stay there. You and those Secret Service agents show up out here, you'll ruin this whole thing."

"Goldang it! You're probably right. So what're you going to do?"

"I doubt I'll have to do much more of anything. The Hollis crowd got together in the newspaper office and I dropped them a note signed 'A Friend' and told them all about the union plan to stop 'em."

"What'd they do about it?"

"I wasn't inside the office, so I don't know the details. I only know they hammered out a plan and they all got their assignments and left."

Alarm sounded in the nasal voice. "Eli, those folks out there don't know what they're up against. Chicago union goons can get rough."

Eli chuckled. "Harry, these folks are just like the ones we both grew up with back home. Feel sorry for the union."

There was a snort and a laugh. "Okay. If you say so. Anybody out there caught on to you yet?"

"Not yet. But there's one thing you better do."

"Yeah? What?"

"Get about fifteen FBI agents into Clarkston, Washington, by morning, any way you can, and tell 'em to stand by for your orders."

"Why do you need FBI agents?"

"Just a hunch. Do it. I'll call you in the morning when I know what to expect."

"You got it. You keep me posted. And you be careful, hear?"

"I will. Give my regards to Bess."

Eli listened while Harry turned in bed. "Bess, Eli sends his regards."

A gentle voice replied, "Give him my love, and tell him he's got to come visit for a week when this is over."

"Eli, hear that?"

"Yep. Tell her she's got a deal if she'll bake some biscuits personally."

He hung up the phone, hitched up his suspenders in the soft, warm air and the deep dusk of a spectacular mountain evening, and drove his pickup back across the river, where he settled onto a stool at the counter in Betty's Pantry and ordered steak and potatoes.

While he waited, he contemplated the next morning's meeting of the cattle truck headed east and the pickup trucks headed west, out near Hollis, and he smiled. Then he chuckled with eager anticipation at the endless possibilities and mental images that came flooding into his mind.

CHAPTER 11

The smooth throbbing of airplane engines overhead reached deep into the slumbering depths of Ollie Whipple's being, and he stirred as the message began its journey to his sleeping brain. A few moments later he listened without opening his eyes and began a count of the number of engines, each with their own individual, identifiable voice.

When he had counted to eight he suddenly sat up on his cot, thrust his head towards the upside-down wooden shipping crate that served as a nightstand, and stared at the luminous green hands on the clock. He had rescued the clock from a wrecked B-17 World War II bomber at the Boise airfield, because the clock had luminous hands that glowed in the dark, and he could see them without turning on the lights.

Ten minutes past four o'clock.

Ollie Whipple was the old caretaker and night watchman at the Lewiston airfield. The World War I U.S. Army Air Corps veteran had three children who were raised and married and gone. Ollie's wife had died from diabetes in 1937. He lived in a small, cluttered room built onto the back of the main office, was amiable, said little, seldom got in anybody's way, and took care of things when nobody else was around.

He jerked the chain on the small lamp beside the bomber clock, stood, reached in the trapdoor on the back of his red, long-handled underwear to scratch, then swallowed at the cotton in his mouth as he walked stiff-legged on the cold floor to the door and entered the main office. He flipped the switch on the radio and waited while it hummed and the lights flickered and came on, and the whine of an unused radio frequency screeched. He twisted a dial to a different frequency and listened intently while a voice came in.

"Ollie, fer cryin' out loud, are you awake down there yet?"

"Tom? That you?"

"Of *course* it's me. I got all my planes up here and there's about ten or twelve others besides. We're gettin' low on fuel, and you better come alive down there or there's gonna be a bunch of holes and wreckage on that airstrip."

Ollie gasped. "What's goin' on? Is that Chicago union sendin' in their air corps?"

"No time to explain. Get Homer on the phone right now, and then turn on every light you got in that building and the hangar, and then get your pickup down at the north end of the field and shine the headlights south."

Ollie grabbed the phone and a sleepy voice said, "Number pleeuzz."

Two minutes later, at their home on the south side of Lewiston, near the river, Nadine shook the shoulder of her snoring husband. "Homer!" she hissed in the black room, "I think the phone's ringin' in the kitchen."

"Huh?" He raised his head far enough to turn on the lamp on the nightstand and squint one eye to study the clock.

"It's barely past four o'clock," he muttered, then stopped to listen to the next faint ring from the kitchen. Two minutes later he stood in his shorts, eyes closed, toes raised off the cold linoleum while he fumbled the earpiece off the phone on the wall by the kitchen back door. In the distance he heard the faint, steady hum of many airplane engines, and he was suddenly wide awake.

"Yeah, Homer speakin'."

"This is Ollie. Tom Bradley's whole outfit's circling the field and there's a big bunch more up there with him. Prob'ly that Chicago union air corps, carryin' machine guns and maybe bombs and stuff. You gotta git here, fast."

Eight minutes later Homer slid his Ford pickup to a stop in the dirt at the south end of the airfield, left the headlights on, sprinted to the main office, and grabbed the radio microphone.

"Tom, you hear me?"

"Yeah."

"The rest of you guys up there, you hear me?"

A dozen voices rang, "Yes."

"I know Tom Bradley's bunch, but who are you other guys? Where you from?"

A dozen voices came back, piling on top of each other. "Chicago. Washington, D.C. Seattle. Portland. Sacramento. Boise. Victoria. Detroit. New York."

Homer's head jerked forward. "Chicago? New York? Washington, D.C.? One of you guys is from Washington, D.C. What's goin' on? Why are all you guys comin' to Lewiston?"

"Newspaper reporter. We was sent by newspapers."

"Holy mackerel," Homer murmured, then took a deep breath. "Okay. Listen close. See them two pickups with the headlights on?"

"Yeah."

"There's about eight hundred feet of dirt airstrip between 'em. Up at the north end there's a mama badger with her younguns' in a burrow, so be careful not to hit it. Come in low over the pickup at the south end, and set down quick and get off the airstrip as fast as you can so the next guy can come in. Tom, you bring your guys in first 'cause you know the airstrip and where that badger hole is. The rest of you guys watch Tom and do what he does. Okay, Tom, do your stuff."

Thirty-five minutes later, with the numberless stars in the black-vaulted heavens fading in the promise of a new day, Homer faced the passengers, who were standing in a group in the hangar. "You guys are all *reporters?*"

"Right."

"Chicago, New York—all them places you said?"

"Right."

"Who sent you here?"

"Chief editor got a call. Said big things were happening out here with a union problem."

"Who called your chief editor?"

"Someone named Clara called mine."

"The woman who called mine said her name's Phoebe."

177

"Our call came from Louise."

"Alice called our main office."

Homer's eyes rolled back in his head. "Oh man! They gone and done it this time." He sobered. "How do you figure to get to town?"

"Does Lewiston have any taxi service?"

"Nope. But give me a minute."

He hurried to the front office and lifted the earpiece from the phone.

"Number pleeuzz."

"Alice, that you?"

"Of course. We're expecting a lot to happen today so I took the early shift."

"This is Homer. You know what we got out here?"

"Airplanes? Newspaper reporters?"

"Twenty-four of 'em, from all over the country. You women got 'em here. You better have some way to get 'em into Lewiston."

"Wonderful. We were expecting them. Someone'll be right out."

"Alice, fer cryin' out loud. When you and the other three get a bee in your bonnets to bring twenty-four airplanes out here in the middle of the night, would you *please tell us?*"

There was a pause before Alice answered sweetly. "Why of course, Homer. Whatever you say."

Five minutes later, six sedan automobiles drove out of Lewiston, headed east towards the airport. They passed the Lumberjack, and Gino, standing with fifteen of his men clustered about, noticed the sedans and for a moment he wondered. And then for the first time he became aware of the heavy stream of pickup trucks

178

moving west into town. He glanced at his watch, then turned his attention back to the men standing before him, dressed in their suits, coats bulging.

"All right, youse guys. Hugo's in charge. Remember, don't show the artillery unless they do somethin' bad."

"Like what?" Hugo asked, shifting the submachine gun stuffed inside the left side of his coat.

"Anything that looks suspicious. Just anything. Remember, you gotta stop 'em from comin' in here to give evidence, and if a fight starts, they gotta be the ones that start it."

Hugo shrugged. "Okay."

The clatter of an old truck engine interrupted and Gino looked down the road at the rusted, dilapidated old cattle truck lurching through the early-morning dusk without headlights. "That's gonna be Tiny with the truck. Him and Dom stopped and lifted them benches from the old schoolhouse for youse to sit on in the back end."

The truck shuddered to a stop with all four brake drums squealing.

"You get them benches?" Gino called up to Tiny through the windowless door.

"Yeah, but Boss, you ain't goin' to believe what's goin' on at the school."

"Like, what?"

"There's about a hunnerd pickup trucks with folks and kids, an' they got picnic baskets, and there ain't no end to the headlights of trucks comin' in at that end of town."

"What they doin'?"

"Just sittin' there."

Gino felt a tinge of concern, shrugged it off, and said, "Okay, load up."

Reluctantly, faces looking like they had been sucking sour pickles, fifteen men walked up the creaking loading ramp and settled gingerly onto the benches, meticulously certain to not touch the green stuff that was so liberally splattered all over the truck. Hugo shoved the loading ramp back onto its rollers beneath the truck bed and walked back to face Gino.

Gino said, "You know the way out there?"

"Sure, Boss." Hugo pointed. "Take this road right out that way and keep goin'."

"Okay. Get goin' and don't come back before dark. I'll have the mediation over by then."

"Yeah, Boss." Hugo went to the far side of the truck, scrambled up into the passenger seat beside Tiny, and moved away from the door frame and braced himself. The door was missing, and both the road and the truck were enough to throw out anyone who was not hanging on for dear life. When Tiny let out the clutch the old truck jumped and bucked, and the passengers in the truck bed cursed as Tiny guided it eastward, out of town.

Gino and Vinnie and the four others who had remained behind to handle the mediation hearing watched for a moment, then walked back into the Lumberjack.

Five minutes later two sedans left town travelling east, staying a mile behind the cattle truck. Norman drove one sedan with Louise beside him and Walt in the backseat with his camera equipment. Clyde drove the other one with Clara seated beside him, tense, eyes glued on the taillights of Norman's car as the yet unrisen sun turned the light skiff of high clouds to an overpowering kaleidoscope of reds and pinks and yellows. And then a tiny arc of sun crept over the rim, and a pristine, unbelievable new day was upon them.

At six o'clock Lou Gibney flipped the switch on his transmitter tower, waited for it to warm up, spun the platter on his turntable, and waited until the last strains of "The Star-Spangled Banner" had faded.

"Good morning everyone out there in happy land. If you haven't heard, the best show in the history of our illustrious mountain Shangri-La is taking place today at the old high school in Lewiston. Take the day off. Grab the kids and some sandwiches. Bring a blanket. We'll push back the green stuff left by Sodderquist's old cow, and I promise you the best show in these parts since Meri set the stakes and Lewiston was built. We're going to have news reporters from all over the U.S. of A., and an army of union witnesses, the sheriff, Norman and Walt from the newspaper, and best of all, Elbert's goin' to be here to help keep this thing movin' in the right direction. If you ain't already done it, get a copy of Louise and Norm's newspaper. Special edition this morning. Remember, you heard it first from me, Lou Gibney."

For eighty miles in all directions, men and women paused, pondered for a moment, and began hasty preparations to inform their bosses, gather their kids, and head for Lewiston.

Twenty-eight miles to the east, Elbert stood on the road next to the Jones's meat plant and raised his hands, and the crowd quieted. They filled the road for fifty yards in both directions, and the dooryard to the old meat plant. Pickup trucks were parked on the road for half a mile in both directions.

"Okay. Everybody understand the plan?"

A swelling chorus answered, you bet, sure, let's get at it.

He turned to Chigger. "Can you and Tank get that old bus out of the river?"

Chigger shoved back the bill of his greasy baseball cap, glanced at his twenty-six-wheeler logging truck, and a grin split the beard on his big, oval face like a melon. "Nothin' to it."

"Okay. You and Tank get goin' right now. The rest of you, follow me. Stop when I do."

Chigger expertly dropped his massive truck into gear and headed west. Then, slowly, like a great winding snake, the file of pickup trucks crept into motion, moving west in Chigger's dust, past Guy Feeney's place, then Kenny Eubanks's place. Elbert glanced to his left when they came to the slope down to the river where he had taken his wild ride to sink the bus. Chigger's truck was already in place, and Chigger grinned and waved him on. Elbert continued to a place where the road ran straight and fairly flat for more than two hundred yards and suddenly he took his foot off the gas pedal.

He leaned forward and his eyes narrowed. "That's them. Right on time."

He stopped his pickup and the mile-long column behind him stopped. One minute later twenty-six men from the first several pickups had disappeared in the rocks and brush and trees one hundred yards north of the roadbed. Elbert got out, grabbed an old, leaky, rusty, five-gallon milk can from the back of his pickup and stood it in the middle of the road twenty feet ahead, then walked another fifty feet and stood in the road, hands on his hips, and watched the cattle truck come to a stop twenty yards away.

The old truck had no windshield, and Elbert could plainly see Hugo and Tiny hunched in the front seat. He dropped his hands to his sides and waited. Hugo climbed through the doorless frame on his side of the truck, walked to the rear of the truck, pulled out the loading ramp, and opened the rear doors. The fourteen irate men inside gratefully made their way to the ground, then walked down either side of the truck to stand near Hugo.

Hugo turned back to Elbert and demanded, "What's all them trucks?" He pointed at the mile-long string of pickups behind Elbert.

Elbert ignored the question. "You're gonna be late for the hearing. Better turn around and get on back to Lewiston."

"We done our evidence yesterday. What's them trucks and folks doin' here?"

"Goin' to town to give their evidence."

Hugo swallowed. "Well, we was sent out here to tell you, your evidence ain't needed. Them folks can turn around and go home and forget it."

Elbert didn't move. "Who sent you?"

The sound of automobiles approaching behind the truck interrupted and Hugo turned around to watch Norman and Clyde stop their cars, and their passengers get out to walk slowly past Hugo and stand silently on the south side of the road. Behind Norman and Clyde, six more sedans stopped, and twenty-four newspaper reporters with little white signs that said "PRESS" stuck in their hatbands clambered out, notepads in hand. Louise had hers, pen poised like a sword. Walt had his big box camera and was fumbling to load it. Clyde slowly pinned his sheriff's badge on his shirt and raised narrowed eyes to Hugo. Behind them, Buster stopped the old mail truck and stepped out and remained beside the door.

Hugo swallowed and Elbert repeated the question. "Who sent you?"

"That mediator guy."

"Louder. I didn't hear you."

"That mediator guy," Hugo said loudly.

"You reporters get that?"

Louise nodded vigorously as she scribbled furiously.

"Hey!" Hugo suddenly bellowed. "What's goin' on here?"

Again Elbert ignored the question. "We're goin' on in to give our side of this whole thing at that hearing."

Hugo felt the beginnings of panic. "But that mediator guy said you wasn't needed."

"You got that in writing?"

"I don't need it in writing."

"Then you better turn that truck around and start back for town." Elbert shifted his feet. "You're startin' to peeve me."

At that moment there was no word in the English language that struck blind terror into Hugo like the word *peeved*, coming from Elbert Pike. Instantly his hand jerked inside his coat and he grasped the handle of the submachine gun.

"Don't you make a move," Hugo shouted. "You just threatened us and we got the right to defend ourselves." He turned and gave a signal and fifteen hands flashed under suitcoats and stayed. The newspaper reporters gasped and moved back two steps, but held their ground while writing furiously the whole time.

"What you got under them coats?" Elbert called. "More guns?"

Hugo did not move or speak, nor did anyone behind him.

"Well," Elbert said, "looks like we better do somethin' about that." He turned his head to the right and shouted, "Kenny, you and your guys cut loose."

It seemed the entire slope north of the road erupted in a one-second, thundering explosion as twenty-six high-powered deer rifles blasted. The dented, rusty old milk can fifty feet behind Elbert jumped clear off the road, tipped in a cloud of dust, and rolled to a stop against a clump of sagebrush. Elbert walked back and picked up the milk can by one handle, walked back to Hugo, and dropped it at his feet.

"There's twenty-six bullet holes in that milk can. If your gang has any ideas about usin' them guns they're holdin' onto under their coats, now's the time."

For three seconds silence hung so thick that they could hear the sounds of the bees and grasshoppers in the wildflowers scattered in the brush on both sides of the roadbed. Not one of Hugo's men moved so much as an eyelash.

Elbert shook his head in disgust. "Just like I figgered." He called up the road to Buster, who was still beside his pickup, behind the truck. "Buster, drive on down here, right in front of this bunch."

Twenty seconds later Buster hauled the old blue pickup to a stop, three feet in front of Hugo's crowd.

"Now you guys lay them guns in that pickup, one at a time, gentle," Elbert ordered, and once again he turned his head to face north and shouted, "Kenny, if any of this bunch makes a move you don't understand, you and your guys cut loose again. Hear?"

A hidden voice came from the slope. "We hear."

Elbert turned back to Hugo and smiled. "You first, nice and easy." He called to Walt, "Get that camera workin'."

Hugo stood frozen and Elbert could not tell whether Hugo's brain was paralyzed or he was purposely defying the direct order. He took one step closer and said, "Mister, I'm gettin' pretty peeved."

Hugo whipped the submachine gun from beneath his suit and had it in the pickup in less than one second while the flashbulb in Walt's camera popped. The others followed.

Elbert nodded approval and called to Clyde. "Come look and see if any of these guns is illegal."

Clyde walked over and peered into the bed of Buster's truck, and turned one of the six submachine guns over. "Yep. Machine guns are illegal. There's six of 'em."

Elbert waved Walt over. "Get a picture of them guns."

The flashbulb popped twice.

Elbert faced Hugo squarely. "Now you're goin' to turn this truck around and we're all goin' back to Lewiston. If you got any other ideas, you better get ready to take on me and everybody in that string of trucks behind me."

186

Two minutes later—with Clyde leading, Norman and Buster right behind, the cattle truck next, the reporters following, and Elbert's mob strung out for a mile—the strange processional started back towards Lewiston.

At eight-thirty Phoebe Nielsen stopped her faded U.S. Mail pickup truck three blocks from the old high school because it was impossible for her to get any closer. Hilda was seated next to her, with Ziggman jammed against the passenger door, while Paul and Hans crouched in the back, holding on to the electronic equipment used for the hearing. People of every description were in the streets, on the sidewalks, all shuffling forward in their efforts to reach the old high school.

"Well," Phoebe said matter-of-factly, "my job was to get you here, and this is as close as we're goin' to get. We'll have to walk from here."

"Heavens," Ziggman exclaimed. "What is wrong with the peoples? Something bad is happening?"

"No," Phoebe answered, "they're just gathering for the show."

"Show? I don't know nothing about no show," Ziggman responded.

"You will," Phoebe said, and got out of the truck.

By five minutes before nine o'clock, Paul and Hans had the equipment ready and Hilda was adjusting the microphones. Ziggman was aghast at the gathering crowd, which now reached as far as his eye could see. The green stuff in the school yard had been shovelled into piles by countless lawn rakes, and blankets were spread with lunch baskets visible everywhere. Children

187

were everywhere a child could get, including two long-legged teenage boys on top of the building, daring each other to jerk the electric dropcord out of the chimney stovepipe.

At exactly nine o'clock Gino and his entourage worked their way through the door and to the front of the room, where they sat down on one of the two remaining benches. Gino looked at Ziggman with a confident smile, pulled out his watch, and asked loudly, "Is it time to start the meeting yet, your honor?"

"Ja," Ziggman responded. "The clock is nine, but Mr. Jones is not here and it would be a mistaken error to taking evidence without him sitting here."

"Your honor," Gino continued, "I have been told by reliable sources that Mr. Jones ain't goin' to be here today on account of he knows he is guilty of all them things we said, and he is heading for Canada so you can't throw him in the slammer. That's what I hoid this mornin' when—"

"They're comin'," a voice sang out, and instantly the room was filled with exclamations. Gino's eyes popped and he looked at Vinnie, then back at Ziggman. "Mr. Mediator, sir, if they ain't on time youse don't have to take no evidence from them and youse can—"

"And here comes them sixteen union guys."

Gino leaped to his feet in disbelief. "What sixteen guys?"

"Yours," answered the voice.

"It ain't possible," Gino exclaimed. "They was sent to stop . . ." He caught himself and stopped short, and Ziggman looked at him with slitted eyes.

Sounds from the crowd outside crescendoed as they opened a path for the incoming group to crowd into the old schoolhouse, and once inside there was no place for any of them to sit. They stood shoulder to shoulder, wall to wall.

From outside came shouts, "There's more comin'. Clyde and Norman and Buster, and about twenny reporters and everybody from Hollis. We got to have more room."

Elbert stood on a chair. "What about we hold this at the city park, where we got electricity and loudspeakers at the band shell?"

The city park was one grassy square block with an old band shell at one end and black loudspeakers screwed to tall posts, where they had summer concerts with the high school band and Mulvaney's Irish string quartet and held the Fourth of July celebration, and square dances on Saturday nights when the weather permitted. Pine and elm trees gave shade and shelter. There were about twenty-five big wooden picnic tables built by the Moose Lodge, and across the street behind the open-faced band shell was an open, six-acre weed patch, bought by the city for parking city garbage trucks but never used because they only had two garbage trucks, and the garbage collectors drove them home and parked them in their driveways at night. Behind the weed patch was an irrigation ditch six feet wide that ran two feet of water throughout the summer, and in which every kid in the city came to wade if they were older, or swim if they were younger, much to the irritation of their mothers, who had to clean them up afterwards.

A deafening roar of approval came rolling from the crowd gathered outside.

Elbert yelled, "Is Burt here?"

Ten seconds later Burt was shoved through the door to face Elbert. "Burt, you're in charge of public works in this town. Can we use the city park for this hearing? There's no way everybody can hear if we hold it here."

Burt swallowed hard, wishing the mayor was there so he wouldn't have to make a decision. "Well, I don't know." He puckered his mouth and scratched his throat. "Maybe, if you pay five bucks."

Ziggman reared up. "You will wait while I am thinking on this. You want to move this meeting down someplace else?"

"Yeah. To the park. Trees and grass."

Ziggman leaned forward intently. "And no more green schtuff outside?"

"No more green stuff outside."

"We move."

Five seconds later someone pressed five one-dollar bills into Burt's hand, and within half an hour the city park was filled to overflowing and the six-acre parking lot was jammed with pickup trucks and a few wagons and sedans. Blankets and kids were everywhere, and mothers were sending irate fathers to the irrigation ditch every twenty minutes to pull their loving offspring out of the muddy water, to bring them back dripping wet and grinning, only to have them break for the ditch again the first time no one was watching.

Half a dozen loggers lifted three picnic tables onto the band shell stage. Ziggman sat at one, with Hilda next to him and Paul and Hans behind him operating the

equipment, which was plugged into the two electric out-
lets. Paul threw the switch, said the word "testing" into
the microphone, and the two speakers blared "testing"
all over Lewiston. Hans reduced the volume.

Gino sat at the picnic table to Ziggman's left, with
Vinnie and his other four. Abe sat with Beth at the
picnic table to Ziggman's right, with Elbert beside them.
Hugo and his army stood on the ground at one end of the
band shell with Kenny Eubanks and twenty-five other
men surrounding them, grinning ear to ear. At one end
of the band shell, leaning against one of the poles on
which a speaker was mounted, the old miner whittled on
a pine stick while he chewed a match and watched, missing nothing. Lined up directly in front of the band shell,
pencils and pads in hands, the twenty-four news
reporters from all over the United States were scribbling
furiously, sketching pictures, intermittently smiling and
laughing.

Ziggman looked at Hilda, who nodded, and he wiped
sweaty palms on his pants legs. He leaned over to the
microphone and began.

"We are now beginning the second day of evidence
in the hearing about the unfair labor charges the union
has said about Abe Jones and the meat company."

The crowd quieted. Ziggman suddenly gained confi-
dence at the sound of his own voice reaching out to half
the town of Lewiston and everyone from Hollis. He
straightened and thrust out his chin.

"The union gave evidence yesterday about assaults
und beatings und drownings in the river. We are here to
taking more evidence." He turned to Gino. "Who will
giving evidence today?"

Gino's brain had gone into gridlock at ten minutes past nine when his sixteen-man army was marched into the old schoolhouse, white-faced and wide-eyed, and he realized his own plan had blown wide open, and worse; if the people who brought them in were allowed to tell the truth, he and his entire entourage stood a fair chance of being in jail by nightfall—or, worse, lynched.

Gino stammered. "Er, your honor, what we got here, we got a witness who's sick. See, Vinnie was going to give evidence today, but he's had a bad sore throat since he got here, and he can't hardly talk."

Ziggman looked at Vinnie. "Is true? You were going to giving evidence and you are too sick?"

Vinnie looked at Gino with eyebrows raised in total surprise, and shrugged. Gino stared at him and nodded his head vigorously. "Yes, sir. Too sick."

Ziggman heaved a great sigh and looked back at Gino. "Who else is giving evidence?"

Gino felt a slight surge of hope. "Well, your honor, Vinnie has to go first, because he's our bookkeeper and he has all the figures on which the rest of us is going to testify and without him first the rest of us hasn't got nothin' upon which to give our evidence. So it looks like we're just going to have to wait a day or two while Vinnie recovers his naturally good health." Gino's eyes were pleading.

Ziggman dropped his head forward while he pondered what to do.

Elbert stood. "Mister, I'm Elbert Pike. Maybe I got an idea that'll help."

Ziggman squared his shoulders and stared at Elbert. "You are Elbow Piker?"

192

Hilda grabbed his sleeve. "Elbert Pike."

"You will please excuse my mistaken error. You are Elbert Piker?"

"Close enough. Yeah."

"You is the one who put the assaults on the bodies of these union witnesses and shoot the window out of the car, kaput, and run the bus in the river to drown these witnesses, and you are working for Abe Jones?" Ziggman looked fierce.

Elbert's face wrinkled while he plowed his way through that one, then he brightened. "Yes, sir, I done all that and I work for Abe Jones."

Ziggman reared back in astonishment. "You admitting all that? That is unfair labor practices and that means we have to slap a huge fine on Abe Jones like two million bucks and close down the meat plant for sixty days. In Germany they don't slap the big fine or close down the business. They slap the bayonets on the rifles and they go finding a wall und . . ."

Hilda grabbed his sleeve.

"We talking about Germany later. If you is now admitting all these bad—"

"Hold on, there," Elbert said. "You look like a fair man. Wouldn't you like to know *why* I done all them things?"

Ziggman straightened, and for long moments he stared at Elbert. Never before had anyone told him he was a fair man, or *asked* him if he would like to know more.

"Ja," he said. "I would like to know why these things happen."

"Swear me in," Elbert said, "and a whole lot of other folks at the same time." He walked quickly to the microphone before Hilda. "All you people we told, raise your hands to be sworn in as witnesses."

Several hands went up all over the park. Hilda swallowed, startled, then repeated the oath over the microphone and a chorus of "I do" came back at her.

"Okay," Elbert started, "we'll start with you, Al. You was at the first meetin' up at Fry's church. What did the union promise us if we joined?"

"Wait a moment," Hilda exclaimed. "The recording machines will not pick up voices out in the audience." Quickly she snatched a shorthand pad and pencil. "All right. Go ahead."

"Go ahead, Al," Elbert called.

"Regular pay even if we didn't work, vacations, sick leave, ten minutes out of every morning to stand around drinkin' coffee. I don't remember all the stuff."

"And who was goin' to pay for all of it?"

"Abe and Beth."

"And who was goin' to pay the union for gettin' all them things from Abe and Beth?"

"Us. Union dues."

A murmur swept over the park.

"Okay Charlie, you're next. You can answer right from there."

Charlie was standing forty feet from the band shell, Evelyn by his side. The nearest person to her on the downwind side was thirty feet away.

Elbert continued. "What happened the day the union guys first showed up out at Abe's meat plant?"

Charlie rose to his one moment of glory. "I was delivering some hams and bacon to Kenny Eubanks from Abe's place when these guys in that black hearse stopped me and unwrapped the meat. I told 'em to stop but they laughed and done it some more. So I come back to Abe's and we re-wrapped the meat and you took it in your pickup and started back to Kenny's with it."

"Thanks, Charlie. Guy, you're next. Did you see what happened the day I blew the window out of that black hearse?"

Guy stood with Emma beside him, holding his hand. "Yessir, me and Emma seen it all. I seen Charlie goin' west in his pickup and then comin' back east, and then you come past in your pickup goin' west again and I followed you. I was right there on the road behind you, and me and Emma seen the whole thing."

"What happened?"

"The hearse stopped you on the road when you was tryin' to deliver ham and bacon to Kenny Eubanks for Abe, and they messed up the meat. One of them guys pulled a pistol and you quickly grabbed your shotgun out of your pickup, and that guy hid behind the back door of the hearse and was fixin' to shoot you, and you blasted that window out slicker'n a whistle, and they all jumped in the hearse and run off. You coulda kilt that guy quicker'n quick but you didn't, you just scared him. That's what happened. Plain and simple."

Elbert called, "Emma, is that true?"

"True as the Bible."

"Buster, you're next. Did you see what happened the day I drove the bus into the river?"

Buster stood straight and tall, and Alice's face flushed with pride and excitement.

"Yessir, I did. So did Norman and Walt and Clyde, 'cause they was right ahead of me. Them guys was drivin' the old Badger school bus out there and stopped you in the middle of the road, and the big one got out and tried to grab you, and you smacked him down and then five more got out to jump on you and you whacked them down, and then the next guy got out with a pistol and you grabbed a pistol from one of the guys that was out cold on the ground and backed the whole bunch into the bus, and then . . ." Buster started to laugh. "The funniest thing I ever seen. Pistols and machine guns come flyin' out the windows of that old bus like rain, and then you jumped inside and next thing I knew, that old contraption was headed for the river, and at the last minute you jumped and the whole shebang went right on in. They all got out, and you taught 'em a bear-scarin' song, and . . ."

Uproarious laughter filled the park and rolled out into the streets of Lewiston. Buster was laughing so hard at the remembrance that tears ran down his cheeks. Elbert let it run for two minutes, then raised his hands and it quieted.

"Go on, Buster. Finish."

"You taught 'em to sing 'We Shall Gather at the River' so they could scare off the bears while they walked all the way back to Lewiston, and they got there at two in the mornin'. Clyde drove ahead of 'em and that's when his car welded into low gear. Them guys sang that song eighty-seven times . . ."

The laughter rose to fever pitch, and Buster was holding his sides and wiping tears at the same time. The twenty-four reporters were hanging onto the front edge of the stage to keep from falling down in laughing fits. Ziggman shouted into his microphone for order, but no one could hear. Elbert grinned for three minutes before he raised his hands and again the crowd quieted.

"Okay, Buster. Clyde, Norman, you heard that. Is it true?"

"Yes, sir. Just like he told it."

"Walt, you was there. You get any pictures?"

"Twenty-six. Here they are." He handed a large brown envelope up to Elbert and Elbert handed it to Ziggman.

"Might want to take a look at those."

Ziggman laid the envelope on the picnic table. "What does bears have with unfair labor charges to do? And singing songs about a river?"

"We'll come to that, but for now let's move on." He turned to Chigger.

"Chigger, did you get the bus out of the river this morning?"

"Yep." He beamed with pride. "Me and Tank. Right over there on my logger."

"Did you search inside?"

"Yep, both of us, just like you asked."

"How many Bibles did you find?"

"None."

"Okay. Clyde, you still got all them guns you gathered up that day when they come flyin' out of the bus?"

"Yes."

"Where are they?"

"I give 'em to Elmer to keep in the back room of his hardware store."

"Elmer, did you bring them guns?"

"Right over there in my pickup, like you said." Elmer's shirt had a sign on the back that said, "Elmer's Hdwe Store—We Got One of Everything You'll Need."

"Buster, you got them guns these guys gave us this morning when they came out to stop us from comin' in here to tell all this?"

"Yep, right over there in my pickup."

"Walt, you got them pictures you took this morning developed yet? The ones of these guys puttin' them guns in Buster's pickup?"

"They're wet, but I got 'em." He handed another large brown envelope with water spots up to Elbert, and Elbert laid it before Ziggman with the first envelope.

"Clyde, you looked at all them guns. Are they legal or not?"

"Twenty-two of 'em are submachine guns, like gangsters use. Illegal."

Elbert looked over the audience for a moment, then pointed. "Maggie, can you hear me?"

"Plain as can be."

"You clean the rooms at the Lumberjack?"

"Every day."

"You clean the rooms where these guys stay?"

"Yessir."

"How many Bibles have you found in there?"

"Bibles? Hah! Only the Bible the Gideons put in every hotel room, and these guys used some pages outta that one to clean up spilt beer."

A gasp swept through the park.

"Iris, you clean up the Aloha?"

"Yes."

"How many Bibles have you found in these guys rooms?"

"None."

Elbert waited for a few seconds while the murmuring stopped, then he slowly walked over to the table where Gino was seated. Gino and Vinnie shrank back, white-faced, and Elbert leaned forward, resting his weight on his stiff arms, palms flat on the table in front of Gino.

"Mister," Elbert said, "I was told you guys swore you were doin' good things at a convent with nuns and orphans, and with Father Flanagan's boys back in Chicago. Is that true?"

Gino looked desperately at Ziggman, then at Vinnie, then at Hugo. He swallowed and said in a hoarse whisper. "Yes. We said that."

"Those is nice things and I hope they're true. So now I'm askin' you here in front of these people. What's the name of the convent, and who is Father Flanagan?"

Gino's face went white, then a pale blue. The pupils of his eyes contracted to pinpoints and he developed a one-thousand-yard stare. His mouth tried to work but sound would not come.

"I'll wait just about ten more seconds, mister, and then I'm goin' to get real peeved."

"Suh-suh-suh Saint Augustine's convent. And Father Flanagan is a Catholic priest at the cathedral. The Saint Jude's cathedral. In Chicago."

Elbert straightened and turned and searched for a moment. "Alice, did you make them calls?"

Alice's face turned red, but she bravely answered, "Yes."

"Is there a Saint Augustine's convent or a Saint Jude's cathedral in Chicago?"

"Neither one. There are four convents, and nine cathedrals, but none of them are Saint Augustine's or Saint Jude's. I got the whole list this morning from Chicago information. Want to see it?"

Elbert handed the list to Ziggman and turned back to Gino and there was fire in his eyes. "You want to explain that, or just leave it alone?"

Gino's jaw trembled and the nervous tick started in his cheek. "Nuh-nuh-nuh no," stammered Gino. "I got nothin' more to say."

The faint tinkle of a bell reached the band shell and for a moment everyone turned to look back at the street. Wally's ice cream wagon had just stopped at the curb. Right behind him came a pickup truck with a sheet of paper stuck in the window with the words "Donuts from Hester's Bakery" spelled out with blue crayon. Hester had tried to draw a donut, but she got the hole off center and it looked like a flat car tire. Hester got out, lowered the tailgate, and the sweet aroma of fresh-baked donuts and sweet rolls came drifting.

Behind Hester's truck, a one-ton flatbed truck squeaked to a stop, and Chuck Wheeler got out and stuck a cardboard box on the top of the cab with CHUCK'S GROCERIES printed on the side in black paint. On the bed of the truck were boxes of bread, lunch meat, potato chips, Baby Ruth candy bars, jaw-breakers, paper cups and plates and napkins, and bottles of cold Orange Crush, Pepsi-cola, and grape soda pop he'd put in his meat cooler overnight.

Kids begged and whined and mothers dug in purses and pockets for nickels and dimes, then turned back to watch what was going to happen next in the band shell.

Elbert stopped for a moment to organize his thoughts, then turned to Ziggman.

"Well, that's pretty much what happened. I'm goin' to bring it all together in real short terms. These guys come to town and tried to get us to help ruin Abe and Beth, and when we wouldn't do it, they got rough. They stopped Charlie and messed with Kenny Eubanks's meat, so I took it and started back to Eubanks's place and they stopped me. They pulled a gun but I got off the first shot and took out the window of their hearse and they ran like rabbits. Then they come out with the old Badger school bus and about twenty of 'em tried to stop me again, and they pulled another pistol. They wound up with all their guns in the road, and them in the river."

Elbert paused for a moment to order his remaining thoughts. "Then they come to these hearings and they done their best to cram you full of stories about their artillery bein' Bibles and such, and they never read a Bible in their lives. They use Bible pages to clean up beer spills. Then they planned to come on out to Hollis and stop us so we couldn't come here and tell you all this, but we heard about it and we come here to set it all straight before you, and we done it. You got twenty-nine pictures there in them envelopes to prove a lot of this, and there's over twenty illegal machine guns in those pickup trucks that these guys brought to town, and we got the sheriff and the newspaper owner and over a dozen other witnesses tellin' you exactly what happened."

Elbert stopped and drew a deep breath before he finished. "I got no idea what all the legal terms are, but I can tell you right now, them guys is liars, and they tried to scare us off with guns, and turn this hearing into a joke. And I ain't about to let that happen, especially to Abe and Beth."

His thoughts ran out and Elbert stopped. It was the longest speech he had ever made. He straightened and looked Ziggman in the eye.

"And now, sir, it's time for you to make a decision in this hearing. Is it over, or do we go on?"

In his entire life, no one had ever given Ziggman such respect, such dignity before an audience as huge as this one. He pushed his gold-rimmed glasses back up his nose and stared for a moment at Elbert.

"I wish to take a little time to thinking about all this so I can do it correct. We will wait one hour."

Elbert nodded and sat down by Abe while movement and noise commenced in the crowded park. Kenny Eubanks waved at Elbert and pointed to Gino's army. They were beginning to move, to push, to try to crowd their way through to freedom, and Kenny's men were setting on their feet, getting ready for a fight. Elbert rose and grabbed Hilda's microphone.

"Elmer, you hear me?"

The crowd stopped milling and quieted.

"Yeah."

"Go on down to your hardware store and round up all the pick handles and axe handles you can find and help Kenny pass 'em out. That bunch of union gorillas thinks they're goin' to make a break for it, and they ain't. I'll see you get paid if any of your goods gets damaged or busted."

Elmer spun on his heel and was gone for ten minutes while the crowd closed in behind Kenny; and five minutes after he returned, Kenny and his twenty-five men had hickory axe or pick handles in their hands and grins on their faces, and the union crowd had stopped pushing.

Eli shoved the whittled pine stick in his hip pocket and quietly slipped away to a gas station two blocks west and dropped a nickel in the slot of the pay phone on the side wall by the air pump.

"Number pleeuzz."

"Long distance. Washington, D.C. Number 2-0-0-0." He waited while circuits clicked and the private, direct line into the oval office rang twice. The nasal voice came on the line, sharp and intense.

"Yeah? Harry here."

"Eli here."

"I know who it is. What's happening?"

"You got those FBI agents gathered at Clarkston?"

"Eighteen of 'em."

"Call 'em right now and tell 'em to get over to Lewiston. Just go where the crowd is. There's twenty-three union guys they need to arrest."

"What charges?"

"Perjury, illegal firearms, transporting illegal firearms over state lines, attempted intimidation of witnesses at a federal hearing, assault, attempted murder, and attempted corruption of an NLRB mediation proceeding."

"Man alive! What's been goin' on? How will the FBI know who the union guys are?"

Eli chuckled. "They're the ones inside a circle of locals carrying axe and pick handles. Tell 'em to find Ziggman and tell him who they are and show their badges. Ziggman's the mediator. He'll help with the bad guys."

Harry broke into relieved laughter. "What happened?"

203

"Read your newspaper in the morning. I'll tell you all about it later. Right now, get those FBI agents moving before these locals come down hard on those union gorillas."

Harry slammed the phone down and Eli walked quickly to the Lumberjack hotel. He waited until the hall was deserted before he again used his key to enter Gino's room. He quickly moved Sacajawea aside while he removed the small microphone from the wires. Then he shoved the whittled pine stick through the hole, forcing the wires into his room on the far side. He pushed the end of the stick until it was flush with the wall, then readjusted the painting and went to his own room. He shaved the end of the pine stick until it was flush with the wall on his side, then wound the wires round the small speaker, and put them and the headset and the microphone under the mattress. Then he walked back out into the bright sunshine of the incomparable day and turned towards the park.

People swarmed and blankets were spread everywhere. Wally and Hester and Chuck sold everything they had and went back twice each for more. Mothers sent fathers to the ditch to recover children drenched with water and mud, scolded their rebellious offspring while they wiped at them with paper napkins, then ducked their heads to grin in the remembrance of the delicious feeling of leaping fully clothed into the ditch in wild abandon, while they watched their kids head right back to the ditch.

At the appointed time Ziggman and his staff resumed their seats on the band shell, and Gino and Hugo were escorted to their place by Kenny Eubanks and two lumberjacks with axe handles, while Elbert sat down by Abe and Beth.

Ziggman waited for the crowd to quiet and then began to speak, haltingly.

"I have taking time to thinking about the evidence. I have looking at the photographs of the bus in the river, and of the guns."

He paused and his eyes took on an unexpected shine while his nearly lipless mouth became firm.

"I have looking at the photographs of the machine guns many times." He held up four photos. "As I have told you, I was raised as a boy in Germany many years ago. I remember the machine guns. Government in Germany was done with machine guns. Hearings was done with machine guns. I was taken to a camp for three years with machine guns and soldiers taught me to use them."

He swallowed hard.

"When I could, I run away from Germany to get away from the machine guns. I came to the United States of America to get away from the brown shirts and the machine guns in the night. Here we do not run our government with guns. We run our government with votes und hearings like this one."

An unexpected hush was settling over the park. Mothers quieted their children and fathers closed their mouths to listen in expectant silence. Half the men in the park had served in World War II. Tank had gotten his name from driving tanks for General George Patton. Chigger had walked through German machine-gun bullets to get ashore at Omaha Beach. Buster had been an ambulance driver. Kenny had taken a bullet through his leg at Tarawa. Jack had been a waist gunner in a B-17 and flown his twenty-five combat missions over Germany. Elbert had volunteered for the marines on December 8, 1941, and cleaned out Japanese machine-gun nests on Guadalcanal until he was wounded and sent home. Charlie had survived mustard gas in the Argonne in World War I. Abe had carried a rifle in the World War I trenches in France. The men quieted in reverent respect and listened as Ziggman continued.

"In this country we hold hearings where anybody can coming to watch and listen, and give evidences. If it is a big hearing, like this one, then we have to hold it in some big places, sometimes in parks, like this one, vit everybody and even childrens running around and making a nuisance and getting wet, and vit ice cream trucks and donuts and bread and baloney. Peoples is allowed to saying what they think is the truth and we hearing both sides and we argue and then we decide."

He dropped his face forward for a moment before he raised it and went on.

"And sometimes we even letting peoples from other countries who cannot talk English so good do these meetings."

Hilda suddenly looked up at Ziggman, her face shining in proud admiration. Elbert bowed his head for a moment before he raised it. Men in the audience looked down at the grass for a moment before they raised their eyes again to Ziggman.

"That is how we do such things in this country. I am vishing I could talk better in English, but I cannot, so I do what I can. I am making mine decision."

He paused, then stood to his full height, a plump, stocky man with a nondescript round face, wide nose, lipless mouth, short-cropped hair, gold-rimmed glasses, and jowls that sagged slightly. His suit was rumpled and his tie was crooked. He looked down at notes he had written, took in a resolute breath, and spoke loud and firm.

"The unfair labor charges against Abe Jones and Beth Jones and their little meat business is fibs. The union who making these false charges is hereby getting three fines. One million bucks for telling so many fibs. One million bucks for trying to stop Abe and Elbow and all others from coming here today to giving evidence."

He paused, and for a moment his jaw trembled. "And one million bucks for trying to do it all with machine guns."

There wasn't a sound as he wiped his eyes for a moment, then took control of himself and continued.

"I wishing I could toss these union peoples in the slammer, but I am only a mediator and I don't got no power to do that. But if I could, I would."

He stopped to glance at his notes, then finished. "And that is mine decision." He turned to Hilda. "Mine good assistant Hilda, with Paul and Hans, will write all this out in English so you can all understand."

He stopped.

A breathless hush had seized the park. No one had been prepared for Ziggman's profound remarks, nor the reach of his decision. Then someone in the park shouted, "That decision don't need no translation. You done just fine, just like it was perfect English!"

Alice stood and hesitantly clapped her hands, and Elbert leaped to his feet and started a thunderous clapping, and then everyone in the park and in the streets was on their feet clapping, shouting, cheering Ziggman.

His jaw dropped four inches. For half a minute he struggled to understand and then he closed his mouth and his face reddened, and he moved his feet and didn't know what to do. He finally nodded to the crowd, and the cheering went on and on until two Greyhound buses stopped on the fringes of the park and eighteen men dressed in neutral colored suits and white shirts and dark ties stepped out and worked their way through to the band shell. The crowd quieted, waiting.

"We're looking for a Mr. Ziggman."

Ziggman looked down at them. "That is me."

"Are you the United States Mediator?"

"Ja."

"I am Randall Waters, FBI agent in charge. These are my men. We have warrants for the arrest of twenty-three men who appeared before you in a union negotiation. Could you point them out to us?"

Ziggman's eyes popped. "Ja." He turned and pointed. "They is right over there, with the peoples and the axe handles all around."

The FBI agents marched their prisoners back to the waiting buses they had rented from the Clarkston bus station, and the crowd applauded and cheered as the buses drove west through town on their way to the Clarkston bridge.

Elbert sighed with relief, then walked to Hilda's microphone. "Folks, it's still early. Got a beautiful afternoon on our hands. Might want to spend the rest of the day right here in the park. I'm sure Chuck and Hester and

Wally got more grub and goodies. Thanks to all of you for coming."

He put the microphone down and instantly LeRoy Tumwald snatched it up. LeRoy owned and operated the Roxy theatre, the only picture show in town.

"Folks, what I done, I rustled up a Roy Rogers and a Hopalong Cassidy double feature, and we got a genuine Movietone Newsreel with Lowell Thomas, and then we got a serial of Flash Gordon, and a Three Stooges comedy and a Mickey Mouse cartoon. The whole she-bang fer ten cents adults, a nickel fer kids, babies free if you'll keep 'em quiet. Family-size popcorn's a dime. We'll run 'em into the night, as long as you'll come to see 'em."

Louise led the news reporters as they stormed Ziggman to copy his decision, word for word, and arrange for copies of all of Walt's photos. No one left the park. The crowd broke into little groups to talk about the mediation, catch up on gossip, and take turns fetching kids from the ditch. Chuck and Hester and Wally went back for their next loads. People came in a steady stream to clap Elbert and Abe on the back, and to shake Ziggman's hand like he had lived there all his life.

Abe worked his way to Elbert and thrust out his big, rawboned hand. "Elbert, I don't know how to thank you."

Elbert grasped his hand, then shrugged. "You're welcome, Abe, but look around. It wasn't just me."

Alice pushed her way to Buster. "Oh, Buster, I'm just so proud of you. The way you got those guns, and talked and all." Her eyes were shining as she blushed and peered up into his face.

"Well, I, . . ." he stammered. "It was you made them calls back to Chicago and made them guys out liars."

"That was nothing compared to what you did."

Buster didn't know what else to say, and he smiled and turned to go. Alice's face fell and her lower lip trembled. Then Buster paused, and turned back.

"Alice, I figger to go see Roy and Hoppy tonight at the Roxy. I was wonderin' if you'd like . . ."

She cut him off. "Oh, Buster, I just positively *love* Roy and Dale and Hoppy."

"Would you like to go? Maybe the midnight show?"

"*Oh, Buster!* I just can't wait! I'll buy the popcorn!"

"Well, no, that's the man's duty."

"But they're serving *family* size tonight. *Please* let me buy, and we can play like family."

A look of wonderment flitted across Buster's face. He knew something in that sentence had gotten past him, and he started back over it, searching.

EPILOGUE

"I *know* what time it is, Ferdie. Get down here *right now*."

Big Ed slammed the phone back on its hook and continued stuffing papers from his desk and filing cabinet into a heavy black briefcase. His frantically packed suitcase lay on a chair next to the open frosted glass door into his private office, sides bulging. He had not shaved nor showered. He wore a suit and a white shirt, but in his blind panic had forgotten his tie.

Ten minutes later he jumped when he heard Ferdie's key in the lock of the outer office door, and he jammed his hand into his coat pocket to grasp the stub-nosed .38 revolver. Ferdie closed the office door and walked on into Big Ed's private office. He slowed while he studied Big Ed, and he noticed the suitcase.

"So what's with the papers in the briefcase, and the suitcase by the door?" he asked.

"You seen the morning papers? Heard the radio?"

"At five o'clock? The papers are just hittin' the streets."

"I got a call from Gino three hours ago."

"Yeah? So?"

"He's in the slammer in Portland! The *federal* slammer, with all the others. All twenty-three. Six different federal felony charges. The FBI got 'em."

Ferdie's mouth dropped open. "What'd they do?"

"Read it for yourself." Big Ed gestured to a four-inch stack of newspapers on a leather sofa against one wall.

"Where'd you get them papers this time of morning?"

"Special wire delivery."

Ferdie spread them out. *Washington Post. New York Times. Detroit Chronicle. Chicago Tribune. Boston Globe. Philadelphia Examiner.* He laid the *Chicago Tribune* flat and froze when he read the two-inch headlines: BIG TROUBLE FOR BIG ED. Beneath it was a twelve-inch-by-twelve-inch photo by "Walt" of eighteen FBI agents snapping handcuffs on Gino and his crowd. In the photo, Gino's face was a study in terror as he shouted, "Big Ed will get us sprung," which words now appeared as the title to the photo.

Ferdie turned the page and stared in disbelief at sixteen photographs of machine guns, the union men in the Clearwater River, a short German reading from notes, a city park jammed with people, and eighteen FBI agents herding the whole union gang into two waiting Greyhound buses.

He started to silently read. Five minutes later he looked at Big Ed.

"Three million bucks." He rounded his mouth and blew air. "It's all over, Big Ed. You had a good run, but it's all over."

Big Ed flashed a weasely grin. "For the union. Not for us."

"You mean that sixteen million?"

"I mean that sixteen million. Took nine years to get it out of that trust fund, but I done it, and I got it in a bank in Rio in a name nobody here ever heard. And I got passports and plane tickets on an 8:10 flight for both of us. You comin'?"

Ferdie shrugged. "Got nothin' better to do. Why not?"

"Anything at your room you want to take?"

"Yeah. A photograph or two, maybe some clothes."

"We'll pick it up on the way to the airport."

"Irene know about this?"

Big Ed stopped. "No. That's why we're leavin' so early, so we're gone before she finds out. I put up with that stupid, bleach-blonde, empty-headed ding-a-ling for seven years of pure torture. I can't stand one more day of her callin' me Eddy Baby, and that whining voice that would clabber milk, and her stupid questions, like how do you spell U.S.A., and those clothes she's nearly wearin'. I woulda canned her the day after she got here except she's the mayor's second cousin and I made a deal with the mayor to hire her if he'd see to it the cops looked the other way a few times. I can't hardly bear the thoughts of even seein' or hearin' her one more time, so let's get out of here."

Big Ed locked the briefcase and Ferdie walked back out into the main office while Big Ed snatched up the suitcase and followed. Ferdie slowed as he approached the front door. Through the frosted glass he could see the dark shape of someone standing outside.

He spoke quietly to Big Ed. "Someone's out there. Got any ideas?"

Big Ed stuck out his jaw and set the suitcase on the floor. He thrust his hand in his coat pocket and settled his finger on the trigger of the revolver. "I got no idea who that is, but we're about to find out. Open the door."

Ferdie turned the handle and jerked it open and quickly stepped aside as Big Ed thrust his hand forward, still inside his pocket, ready to fire the pistol.

"Eddy Baby!" Irene stood with a suitcase in either hand, her twenty-inch, floppy-brimmed red hat pinned to her head, a green velvet sheath dress slit up the left side to her thigh, and a mink stole draped over her shoulders.

"Ready to go?" She smiled, and tiny flakes of makeup drifted down to the green dress.

Big Ed gaped, speechless. Ferdie raised both eyebrows to watch.

"Plane's leaving," Irene said.

"Go *where?*" Big Ed stammered.

"Rio. I got my ticket and passport, same as you."

"Who told you?"

Irene shrugged. "A girl knows these things. We better get movin'."

Big Ed exploded. "You ain't goin'! I put up with your whinin' and stupidity as long as I can, and there ain't no way I'm goin' to stand it for one more day. Do what you want. Go where you want. Just stay away from me! Understand?"

Irene's black eyebrows peaked. "Eddy Baby, you do me pain. I gave you the best years of my life and I kept secrets for you, and now you do me pain. You oughtn't do that while I got the books."

Big Ed gasped. "What books?"

The ones on that sixteen million you got in Rio under that new name. Let's see. What was it? Oh yeah."

She smiled sweetly. "Archibald Worthingham. Like in England."

Big Ed's eyes glazed and several seconds passed before he blurted, "You ain't got no books on that sixteen million because there ain't no books."

"Oh, no, not the books on the sixteen million. The books from which the sixteen million was stolen. Vinnie had 'em. Now I got 'em. And you *know*, you just absolutely, positively *know* I wouldn't never let the feds see those books."

"You got 'em? Where?"

"At a bank in Rio in some sort of box. I fergot what they call it. Safety deposit box? Is that what they call them boxes nobody else can get in? Us dumb, air-headed, bleach-blonde girls who can't spell U.S.A. have a hard time rememberin' things like that, right?"

Ferdie looked at the floor for a minute, then grinned.

Big Ed stood in shock like his feet had grown to the floor.

Irene smiled sweetly again, and more tiny white flakes sifted onto the green velvet dress. "Come on, Eddy Baby. We got to hurry if we're goin' to catch the 8:10."

ABOUT THE AUTHOR

Ron Carter was born in Salt Lake City and raised in Twin Falls, Idaho. He served a full-time mission to Norway, and went on to receive a bachelor's degree in industrial management from Brigham Young University. He received a juris doctor degree in 1962 after attending the law schools at George Washington University and the University of Utah. Recently he has been a research and writing director for the Superior Court system of Los Angeles County, California.

The author published his first work in 1988, and has since published two volumes in the acclaimed *Prelude to Glory* series, as well as *The Trial of Mary Lou, The Blackfoot Moonshine Rebellion of 1892,* and *The Royal Maccabees Rocky Mountain Salvation Company.*

He is married to LaRae Dunn Carter of Boise, Idaho, and they are the parents of nine children. The family resides in Claremont, California.